Robbery in Savage Pass

When a Pinkerton agent offers Soames Ho the job of taking gold from Marysville to a Californian bank he accepts. The stagecoach carrying the gold travels through Savage Pass with a nervous driver and a greenhorn shotgun rider. Waiting up ahead are three men intent on robbery.

The Pinkerton agent has deliberately set it up so that no one with guts or real fire power escorts the stagecoach, but he got Soames Ho all wrong. Soames believes in justice and, whatever the cost, he is determined to find the gold and the outlaws.

Robbery in Savage Pass

D.M. Harrison

A Black Horse Western

ROBERT HALE · LONDON

© D.M. Harrison 2010
First published in Great Britain 2010

ISBN 978-0-7090-8940-7

Robert Hale Limited
Clerkenwell House
Clerkenwell Green
London EC1R 0HT

www.halebooks.com

The right of D.M. Harrison to be identified as
author of this work has been asserted by him
in accordance with the Copyright, Designs and
Patents Act 1988

Typeset by
Derek Doyle & Associates, Shaw Heath
Printed and bound in Great Britain by
CPI Antony Rowe, Chippenham and Eastbourne

CHAPTER ONE

Everyone could see that the man had something about him which discouraged questions from all but the foolish. It could've been the slight upward turn of his eyes, or the severe line of his mouth, or the frown etched into his brow, or perhaps it might have been the three wounded men who crawled in front of him as he rode into town that made him look so mean.

He looked a hundred years older than his twenty-five years.

The town marshal raised one querulous eyebrow at the sight.

'What you got there, feller?' he asked.

Soames Ho, the man in question, dismounted his horse and pushed one of the men towards the marshal. He carried his shotgun open to show the barrel, now empty of ammo. He'd ceased to need a gun to sweep the trash into town. He'd already tamed them.

'These men came onto our homestead.' His black-booted foot aimed at the butt of another man and sent him sprawling at the feet of the marshal. The third man moved out of reach, but not too far, because the young man had loaded pistols in his belt. 'These three raped and killed my ma and sister.' Soames Ho turned his head towards the second horse which had two bloodied bodies laid across its back. 'Those two murdered my pa,' he said.

A crowd of people had now gathered round. News travelled fast in the town. No one said a word; they just listened to the story Soames Ho had to tell. They knew the Ho family had lived in these parts for almost a quarter of a century. The grandparents had left China and settled in America. Soames's father had married an American girl hence the young man's slightly oriental appearance and inscrutable manner.

The marshal shook his head.

'I'm sorry to hear that, son.' He looked at the cowering, bloodied men. 'How is it that you're standing tall with not a scratch on you?'

Soames Ho nodded. 'That's a fair enough question,' he said. He scratched his head and pondered the question. Then he pushed back the spirals of glossy black hair which escaped from under the broad-brimmed hat before he spoke again. 'Seems these fellers thought I'd be away for the day. And I would've too, but my horse went lame and I returned home to find them making free with my family. I had to wait and pick them off one by one.'

His eyes glazed over momentarily as the scene paraded before him inside his numbed mind. He saw the torn petticoats, the bloody, broken bodies of his ma and sister. His pa, tortured out of recognition. The men, drunk as skunks, still managed to shoot holes in him. He forced the images away.

He moved towards the bodies on the horse, untied the rope that secured them, and unceremoniously allowed them to fall to the ground.

'These two varmints put up a bit of a fight.' His mouth curled at the corners in a grin, like he was enjoying a private joke. 'They didn't live to tell you the tale.' He kicked at them, as if to make sure they were dead. 'But I've brought the others in to make sure they pay for their crimes.'

'You best tell me all that happened before you leave town,' the marshal said. He had no doubt that Soames Ho had told the truth. The family had lived here for a long time. They didn't mix much with other folk, kept themselves to themselves. But they were good people who'd help anyone out. Perhaps that had been their downfall, the marshal wondered.

'Don't worry, I'll be around long enough to see them swing,' Soames Ho assured the marshal.

The men who'd survived Soames Ho's vengeance were now locked good and tight in the town's jail. They'd never escape from there, the law man had assured Soames Ho. They stood before a building built solidly of schist rock firmly set in mortar. To make doubly sure the marshal had fastened the prisoners by leg irons into the heavy ring set in the centre of the jail.

Marysville, a town which had grown on the back of the gold rush era, had moved from using a hanging tree to a purpose-built scaffold. Soames Ho listened to the nails as they were banged, one by one, into the wood. He stood in the saloon and drank the house whiskey, savouring every thump of the hammer.

The three men had been found guilty at their trial; they'd done a lot of things, apart from the carnage at the Ho homestead and they'd soon all do a dance macabre on the end of a rope.

'So what are you going to do now?' Lode Pinkerton asked.

He'd invited Soames Ho to sit down and share a bottle of whiskey with him. The large bulky man puffed and wheezed out the words. His bulbous, pitted nose told of his fondness for alcohol. He poured the whiskey into the other man's glass and refilled his own.

Soames Ho drank slowly and considered the question.

'I think I might move on,' he said.

'I suppose I'd do the same,' Pinkerton agreed. 'My second cousin, Allan Pinkerton, is always looking to recruit men like you. He's set up a detective agency.'

Soames Ho pointed to his belt. It was bereft of guns. 'I've done with violence. As soon as I've seen the three men swing from the hangman's noose, that'll be all the violence I want.'

'No,' Lode Pinkerton assured him, 'he doesn't want gunslingers. All my cousin wants is people who can ask the right questions and bring criminals to justice.'

Soames Ho shook his head. But Pinkerton persisted. 'There's a job coming up,' he tapped the side of his nose, lowered his voice conspiratorially as he looked round to make sure no one else listened to the conversation, and squinted through watery eyes that were almost lost in the flesh of his face. 'There's a stagecoach going from here to San Francisco and it only needs a man who'd make sure a box of gold got signed in at the bank.'

Soames Ho said nothing.

'It's an easy job. And once the gold is in the bank

that's it. You've earned yourself a free passage to San Francisco.'

'So you want me to be the shotgun rider?' Soames Ho asked.

Pinkerton shook his head. 'No, you're just an observer, nothing more.'

'I'll give it some thought,' the young man agreed.

'It goes at the end of the week,' Pinkerton said.

'Soames Ho,' the marshal said after the outlaws were finally found guilty, 'it seems there was a large reward for those men, dead or alive.'

He'd called the young man into the law office after their conviction. As they stood together the marshal put $1,000 on the table.

Soames Ho pushed his hands deep into his pockets of his brown wool pants as if he was frightened to touch the stuff, and stared at the man as if he'd given him a pile of horse dung instead of a bag of money.

'I don't want it,' he said.

'I'm only doing my job. You take it,' the marshal insisted.

Soames Ho eventually picked up the money as if it would bite. He carried it down Main Street towards the schoolhouse. It was a wood-framed building covered with adobe sundried brick and wood, based on thick rock foundations. It was a place that looked as if it ought to stay there forever, yet its roof was mean and the iron window shutters were missing more than a hinge or two. The sound of children's voices floated towards him. As he stepped into the doorway of the schoolhouse the sound fizzled out and Annie Greaves, the teacher, quietly dismissed the class. The sound of thirty pairs of feet clattered down the steps of the schoolhouse.

Alone with the young woman at last, Soames Ho touched the brim of his felt hat, and then removed it. He acted respectful towards the teacher. As he placed the money into her hands, her pink bow mouth turned up at the edges and she raised china-blue eyes towards him. Although his face remained outwardly immobile, he swallowed hard and wondered when teachers got this good to look at.

'Mr Ho, I can't take all this money,' she said.

'I guess you could do a lot of good with this. The school is the heart of the town. I ain't a philosopher, miss' – he nodded towards the jailhouse – 'but maybe the more education these youngsters get, perhaps it will help keep them out of there.'

Annie Greaves smiled. 'I think you're right, Mr Ho. Thank you.'

Soames Ho put on his hat again and turned to leave but Annie called out to him.

11

'Will you come back again to see how the money is spent?' she asked.

Soames Ho pulled the brim of his hat down against the sun.

'I ain't sure of my plans yet, miss, but I'm sure you'll spend it well.'

First though, before he did anything else, Soames Ho went back to the smallholding he'd lived on all his life. It wasn't the same now and he felt he couldn't settle there again. Also on the surface there seemed little reason to say no to the stagecoach trip to the west coast. And as Lode Pinkerton had said, if he didn't want to be involved with the agency, he'd still have had the free passage to San Francisco. It seemed an easy job. What could go wrong?

Soames Ho had one more job to do before he could move on. He buried his pa and ma and sister, Honey, on a hill which overlooked the homestead and the town. Soames Ho hoped they'd remember the good times they'd had there and forget that one terrible day. Friends and townspeople stood in silence as the preacher said a few words over the graves. They left as Soames Ho walked around the homestead once more. He rubbed his eyes at the sight of the Trees of Heaven which populated the place. His grandfather, whose efforts at mining had rewarded the family with a comfortable home, had brought the seeds over from China. It was a sentimental reminder of the past. Soames Ho shook the memories away. His time to grieve was over.

On Friday morning, as three bodies swung in the breeze, Soames Ho, all neat in a dark wool suit, white shirt, black boots and a small valise, said goodbye to his homestead and Marysville and joined the stagecoach to San Francisco.

CHAPTER TWO

The four horses shied and snickered in alarm. Perhaps they smelt trouble in the air as they threaded their way through Savage Pass.

Every so often a metal hoof slipped and grated across the rocky path as they placed their feet gingerly onto the ground. Dan Buckon shushed the horses, hissing through his yellow teeth in a gentling way. He had years of experience at quelling disturbed beasts. He smelt the same fear as they did and wiped the sweat from his brow with a white spotted red kerchief his wife had bought him then pushed it back into his cotton shirt pocket. His shaggy hair, too long for the heat of the summer, stuck like rope to his head.

He hunched his old body protectively forward on the buckboard and wished that the journey, or at least this part of it, would soon be over. Miles Tay, the young shotgun at his side, sat upright, his thin wiry body taut with anticipation with hair that seemed to spike up with the excess energy he generated. It threatened to push the wide-brimmed hat clean off his head.

Dan thought it a good thing Miles's pants were reinforced with buckskin or they'd be full of holes the way he squirmed around on his seat.

It was Miles's first ride as guard. He'd been hired by Wells, Fargo and Co to take the miners' gold from Yuba County, through to San Francisco, California. This was his first real job. He'd practised shooting on his pa's farm and he could hit a line of tin cans so fast they'd fly into the air and be smashed by the force of the bullets. One even flew so high it knocked a bird right out of the sky and his ma served it up for supper. Or so Miles said. And everyone in town knew he was good at bragging even if he didn't shine at much else.

Dan wished the company had chosen someone with more experience to sit on that dark-green strongbox of gold. The young dude was far too bristly and trigger happy. Dan expected him to be popping at shadows before they got through the pass.

And there were passengers to think about. A couple of gals, Mae and Tootsie, from the saloon, off to make a decent life in San Francisco, or so they said. Dan thought there wasn't much chance of anything for a woman unless she could get a good catch. Maybe they'd do all right out there, if they pretended to be widow-women and left the bad days behind them. Old Mrs Ryder, off to visit her sick aunt, sat well away from the gals, as if she'd get infected by their presence. Dan chuckled at the thought that Mrs Ryder had been doing the same as those gals, only difference was she'd got a gold ring on her finger.

There was a man aboard as well. He sat quietly in the corner of the coach, socializing with no one although he was polite enough to the ladies. The marshal told Dan the man had recently lost all his family and that probably accounted for his reserved manner. He had a slightly oriental look about him, but Dan thought it was perhaps the way he stared intensely when he asked a question. He was something to do with the company, he believed.

Dan couldn't wait to get through Savage Pass and out to the other side. Wasn't called Savage Pass for nothing, he mused. It was stark, foreboding and full of crevices, carved out of sandstone, in which to hide. The path through was narrow all the way, and sometimes you looked over and saw a sheer drop. Dan was glad the passengers didn't have the same view as him with his elevated position or he'd have ladies who'd scream fit to bust and faint on him. Trouble was, he'd have to leave them to get on with it. No way would he stop in this damn awful place.

Dan finally came upon the place he found no favour with, and just the thought of it raised goose bumps over his skin. The spot was always bad but at this time of year, the trees, in full leaf, overhung the route and made it worse. You couldn't have spied a buffalo in the branches let alone a squirrel looking for nuts to last over the winter. A nasty thought that always came into Dan's head sprouted up again.

'A whole gang of outlaws could be hidden up there,' he whispered.

Miles held his shotgun tight in both hands. He swung the weapon back and forth as he looked out for hidden dangers.

'Hold on with that thing, boy,' Dan grumbled. 'Don't want my head blown off.'

He shook his head. It couldn't be long before the gun went off, he thought. Any minute now that thing would be spewing pellets like popcorn at a picnic. He pulled the brim of his hat down over his eyes to protect them from the sun, and hoped he'd still have a head left to hang it on when the journey was over.

The strongbox under Miles Tay's feet fairly burnt a hole through his black leather-soled boots. The wood seemed to pulse with the brightness of its contents. A part of him knew he was being fanciful, and he wasn't usually prone to such vivid imaginings, but the job, given to him by the company had gone to his head. He'd been given a fair amount of responsibility and it was a big jump from farm boy to shotgun.

Truth was, Joe Ferns, the usual man to ride out with Dan Buckon, had a bad belly that gave him a big dose of the back-door trots and he couldn't get himself out of the outhouse. He'd been there a few hours after eating a bowl of pork stew. A heavy dose of spices had camouflaged the fact that it stunk before it got to the cooking pot. Joe cursed Moley Griffin's Diner and, if he could just heave his backside from the privy seat, he'd turn Moley Griffin into the next dish on the menu. So faced with no one else being available, the company had accepted the first feller to volunteer to ride in Joe's place.

Dan couldn't stop shaking his head at the company's choice, but they only paid him to drive and didn't give a plug nickel for his opinion. He shrugged his shoulders, after all they hired him and his stagecoach to take mail and goods and nothing more.

He just did his job.

CHAPTER THREE

Waiting up ahead were three men. Two were in the cover of the overhanging trees. They caught the sound of the stagecoach and knew it would soon be time for them to move.

One man, Sirrus Warman, had stopped looking for his own gold a few years ago. He'd joked it was because he found it too much like hard work and that wasn't far from the truth. He liked the easy life and hadn't found it toiling in the streams and rocks; always looked like the man further down the stream or in the next mine along found a strike whilst his tin pan remained empty. To him everyone else got lucky. As he sat mulling over his mug of whiskey, he had failed to notice that the others, with 'all the luck', were still working.

Sirrus tugged his long and straggly yellow

moustache, a colour completely opposite to his head of dull-brown hair, which added to his perpetual hang-dog expression, and hoped he'd do better this time and get some money.

His rough cotton, light-blue shirt scratched his skin. No matter how many times he hung it out to air, and it got wet with rain to wash the grime away, the material never lost its rough feel. Now, together with the patched overalls, it made him feel like he'd got a nest full of ants which had taken to crawl all over him. He sniffed the odour of his hat, and regretted soaking it in oil to make it waterproof. Dang stunk in the heat, he cursed, and smelt like something had curled up on the top of his head and died.

All he knew was that he was bored and uncomfortable as he waited for the dang coach to come along. He thought this, but he kept it to himself, sure he'd find the other man unsympathetic to his plight.

He looked across to see if he could see his companion, Joaquin Mateo, a half-breed Mexican, who had a chip on his shoulder big enough to fill a woodshed for a whole winter. Joaquin had boasted that his soldier father hadn't hung around long enough to teach him to shoot, but the survival instinct had passed through with his genes. He believed he'd killed enough men to make his father proud.

They sat either side of the ridge above Savage Pass and waited for the stagecoach to come through. Joaquin had heard the miners were sending a box of gold through the pass today.

'Seems like they decided no one would notice a small stagecoach. Perhaps they thought we'd never guess there was anything worth taking,' he'd told Sirrus.

'So how come you know?' Sirrus queried.

Joaquin had only tapped the side of his broken nose on a battle-scarred face, as if to signal he knew and that was enough. A man of few words, he'd said all he was going to say on the subject.

Sirrus Warman could see the big, mean shadow that was Joaquin Mateo. The black outline silhouetted the actions of the man. He watched as Joaquin pulled his guns from their holsters to inspect them. Peacemakers, Joaquin called the .44 Colts but Sirrus knew he never made peace with those things. They were in good working order; he'd killed a man once because the fool thought he could insult Joaquin Mateo. The half-breed was a bastard in both name and nature, but he didn't let anyone call him that. He said it as a joke, but no one laughed.

He knew his friend's fingers would soon be clasping and unclasping the trigger of the shotgun he carried in anticipation of the robbery.

21

And he knew he'd made a bad mistake when he'd teamed up with Joaquin Mateo. His companion thought nothing of killing. Last night Sirrus had seen him shoot a man he'd accused of cheating when he'd lost in a poker game. He got a bullet straight through the eye. It had turned out the man was honest. But no one said anything about the incident; that is, no one who wanted to stay in his skin for the full length of its natural lifetime.

Absent-mindedly, he pushed his upper teeth into his lower lip and almost started at the pain of the action.

Sirrus rubbed at the foot he'd pushed into the crevice of the rocks he leant against to stabilize his body. It was a cramped position to hold. A pebble fell when he moved and the sound it made as it fell down Savage Pass was as loud as an avalanche. He cast his glance across to Joaquin Mateo but nothing moved over there. Sirrus gave a sigh of relief. Perhaps it had sounded louder than it was.

Joaquin Mateo spat out the tobacco and silently cursed the other man. The fool might as well stand up and shout 'I'm here'. He kept his ears open for any reaction in the pass. Nothing. He relaxed. Even if the people on the stagecoach became alarmed, there was no way they could turn back. They were past any turning places now. This was the straight route down. It was as though he, Sirrus and Bart were the spiders waiting for the fly.

Bart Ford, the third one in the trio, lay in wait further up the pass. He could pick any off that escaped from Joaquin or Sirrus. Not that anyone would, Joaquin smiled, he'd make sure of that.

Joaquin Mateo had the best vantage point and as soon as the stagecoach came into view, he'd give Sirrus and Bart the nod and they'd both slide down the slope, Bart a little way back, but all with guns ready to fire. He knew that to jump out might scare the horses and they could shy and bolt off, but it was a calculated risk. Joaquin knew that if they tried to get through the narrow gorge they'd not get far before they either stopped or broke a leg.

Either way the spoils from the stagecoach would be theirs.

He worried about Sirrus. The man was nervous, tugging on that moustache fit to pull it off and biting at his lower lip till it almost drew blood. He shook his head as he recalled the way Sirrus had fretted over the robbery. 'Suppose someone gets hurt?' he'd asked. Didn't the feller realize they weren't going on no Sunday picnic? If you took someone else's gold then chances were you'd face a bit of trouble.

He hoped the trouble wouldn't include the man who was in his gang. He didn't want to have to kill the feller but he'd lose no sleep if he did.

Joaquin Mateo looked up the slope towards the third man, Bart Ford, who accompanied them. He had no qualms about this man; felt he'd been carved from the same tree. He'd proved capable enough times before. Mistake Joaquin realized he'd made was to ask Sirrus Warman to join them.

Joaquin chewed on a fresh plug of tobacco and waited.

Bart Ford's eyes flickered in acknowledgement of his companions. They were eyes that were black and merciless. He, too, scoffed at Sirrus Warman's fears. He recalled that he'd asked if people would get hurt and a rumble of silent laughter shook his belly. No one ever got left hurt when he, Bart Ford, was around.

That's because he always left them dead.

CHAPTER FOUR

Stray leaves, which blew in the light wind, fell onto Dan Buckon's hat but he merely brushed them aside. Miles Tay, on the other hand, tensed; his finger itched to tighten on the trigger. He pulled at the now too-tight collar of his once crisp, starched shirt. Except for the collar, it hung limp with sweat over his body.

The further into this ride they travelled, the more Miles wondered whether he'd done the right thing taking this job.

Had he ventured to say his thoughts out loud to Dan, the old boy would've creased his fat face into their well-worn laughter lines and told him it was far too late to worry now. As it was, Miles had the answer less than a few moments later. It hadn't been a sensible thing to do. He should have stayed on the farm with his pa and ma.

From either side of the trunks of the trees, two men, with masks that covered their lower faces, jumped out. Dan Buckon, together with Miles Tay, looked down the barrels of two shotguns.

Dan immediately knew that the long journey they'd started this morning was about to get a lot tougher. A thin scream escaped from the back of the younger man's throat and emerged as a whistle which pierced the ears.

'Shut that racket up.'

The sounds were loud in the now silent afternoon. It seemed as if the birds had stopped in mid-song and even the creatures in the undergrowth had turned the volume down.

However, the horses, spooked by the strangeness of it all, strained wildly at their harnesses. Four sets of huge eyes bulged out of their heads in terror.

'Easy now,' Dan called out softly to the team. He pulled on the reins to bring them under control again. Eventually they calmed and apart from a hoof scraping at the floor and a snort of fear, they stood still with their driver above them.

'Come down from there,' Joaquin ordered. His voice sounded muffled under the kerchief. 'Put your guns down and take it nice and slow.'

'What on earth is going on?' Mrs Ryder stuck her

head out the coach window.

'Get back in there, Missus.'

Mrs Ryder, frozen in position at the sound of the voice, merely continued to stare. Joaquin Mateo raised his gun and fired. He aimed one bullet at her and then at the wheel of the stagecoach. As the coach fell at an angle, one of the gals inside pulled the older woman out of range of another bullet. They had enough sense to keep themselves hidden.

Inside the coach Soames Ho stayed put.

Perhaps he'd decided that he ought to protect the women, Dan thought. But he didn't have time for many more thoughts. What happened next took place in a short few seconds. Everything got measured out in slow motion.

It started with Miles who didn't take kindly to being told he was going to be parted from the wooden box beneath his feet. His first reaction of fear towards the outlaws got forgotten as anger took over. The expression on his face said it all. No way he'd let those *hombres* take what didn't belong to them. He reckoned he was fast enough to take them all out.

Joaquin Mateo and Sirrus Warman weren't tin cans standing on a fence. As Miles pulled the trigger of his shotgun, the 'tin cans' reacted faster than any he'd ever shot at.

Miles Tay looked down. A stupid, glazed look filmed over his eyes. His hand moved towards the red patch that appeared on his chest then started to spread over and cover it completely.

'Hell, this shirt feels wet.'

Those were the last words he said to Dan after the blast from Joaquin Mateo's gun lifted him upwards from his seat. The young face squinted with pain and his short life flashed before his eyes. He was dead before he hit the ground.

Dan on the other hand had lived a lot longer on this earth. He'd hoped to see out his days sitting by a hot stove in the general store, drinking coffee and smoking a clay pipe with his cronies and going home each night to taste his wife's home-made apple pie. He slowly put his hands in the air as he watched Miles tumble from his seat.

Unfortunately, he wasn't slow enough to suit Joaquin. Jittery from the boy's unexpected reaction, he pulled both his guns from their holsters and fired. Dan's hat blew right into the air as he became the second person to see his life flash by. He only got as far as meeting his wife at a Sunday hoe down. Then his head dissolved into a splatter of red and white chunks and his hat settled back down onto his shoulders before falling over the side to join Miles Tay.

The noise of the gunshots reverberated around the pass before it became silent again. Then the three men stared at one another as Bart Ford joined them and the sound of his laughter woke the pass again.

'Did you see that?' he howled.

The women in the stagecoach took their cue from this and a cacophony of screams assaulted the ears of the men. A black-winged bird launched itself from a high rocky ledge. The beat of its wings added to the noise.

Joaquin Mateo put his hands to his ears and then rushed over to the stagecoach. Bart Ford aimed his gun at it.

'Please be quiet, ladies.'

The entreaty came from the man inside the coach.

Soames Ho wanted to fight the three men, but he was unarmed and vulnerable. And the three women needed him to remain calm.

It was the first time the robbers had noticed the oriental man, but Joaquin Mateo didn't see him as a danger. He continued to threaten the passengers. He didn't raise his voice. He kept it cold.

'You'd betta take your gentleman friend's advice. I could let my trigger-happy friend shoot you all. Or perhaps I ought just to push this thing over the other side of the ridge.'

'I think the ladies are all right now,' Soames Ho said.

Joaquin Mateo spat in disgust and turned away. 'They'd better be,' he said.

Then silence ruled Savage Pass once again.

CHAPTER FIVE

Sirrus Warman had stood by, almost mesmerized by the two deaths that had taken place before his eyes, and all in the space of less than five minutes, but the threat of more to come galvanized him into action.

'What have you done?' he asked incredulously.

Joaquin Mateo merely shrugged his shoulders. Bart Ford sneered in the horrified man's direction. Neither seemed to think an explanation was warranted, so why waste words? They ledged their shotguns near the trees and moved towards the green strongbox underneath the shotgun rider's seat. Then Joaquin felt a hand grip his shoulder.

'You've killed two men,' Sirrus spluttered.

Joaquin's hand moved to the gun in his holster.

His hand settled on his .44.

'Be careful, my friend,' he hissed at Sirrus. 'You could end up like these two.'

He dropped his hand from Joaquin's shoulder.

'I never agreed to this.'

'You ain't criticizing us, Warman?'

Bart Ford squared up to Sirrus and dared him to say some more. His two black eyes glistened with evil as he stared the other man out. Sirrus backed away but then he saw Joaquin Mateo spit in the direction of the two bodies and he saw red.

He didn't consider the consequences of his actions as his fist smashed into the side of Joaquin's jaw. For once the man was unprepared. He hadn't been ready for Sirrus's reaction. It stunned him, but not enough and he fought back sending a punch into Sirrus's diaphragm. Sirrus, winded for a moment, fell back and stumbled onto the path.

The horses snickered and whinnied in distress. They couldn't move with the broken coach, but they had no hand to guide and control them now Dan was dead and they tried to bolt. The front horse reared up onto its hoofs, lifting itself into a standing position.

Joaquin Mateo laughed as Sirrus Warman fell dazed on the ground. He quickly reached for his shotgun, reloaded and took aim.

'Goodbye, *amigo*. You were always too much trouble.'

Bart Ford looked on, irritated by the scuffle; he hadn't got time for this and told them both to hold off.

'You boys can fight until you knock each other into a cocked hat when we've got this over with,' he said.

Sirrus didn't hear Bart. He waited for the shot that would send him to hell. He screwed up his eyes tight and held his breath. The bullet never reached him. The horse's hoof caught Joaquin's hand as the animal came back down from its frightened stance and the iron shoe that hit bone made a crack like a gunshot. For a moment, Sirrus thought he was a goner and waited for the pain and then oblivion to come.

When the expected didn't come, he opened his eyes again. He saw Joaquin fall forward towards him with his face concertinaed in pain. Immediately, Sirrus brought his foot up, kicked out hard, and as it made contact with the other man's jaw he heard a crunch. He watched Joaquin, face full of blood and teeth, slip and fall. A scream rent the air as he tumbled down the very ravine he'd threatened to throw the women over. Sirrus watched as Joaquin went over and over until he hit the ground. Then there was no movement at all. Not even a twitch. He lay still and all was eerily silent again. Sirrus felt the women were holding their breath, waiting for their end to come. Three people were dead.

Bart Ford stared in disbelief at the scene that had been played out in front of him.

'And now there are two of us. . . .'

His hand went to his gun in his belt as Sirrus Warman rolled away and grabbed a shotgun. Bart was faster. He aimed his gun at the centre of Sirrus's head before the man had a chance to reload.

'And then there was one. . . .'

Sirrus just wanted to get out of this situation as fast as possible. He looked at the man with the gun and then at the gold. As far as he was concerned Bart could have it all. But he had to persuade Bart Ford not to shoot him first. He was a gone goose if he failed to convince him how much he needed him.

'Bart, you'll never get this box up the hill without me,' Sirrus said.

Bart kept his gun aimed at a spot on Sirrus's head for an agonizing moment before finally lowering it. His face had puckered like a wet sheepskin before a fire but then he eased up some, as if he could see sense in Sirrus's words.

'Don't get your back up,' Bart said. 'We need to stick together.'

They went back to the stagecoach and took the strongbox. When the women saw them approach, they must have thought the men were after them, because they started to scream again. As Sirrus struggled with the heavy strongbox he wondered if he should try to reassure them. Bart had no such qualms and he threatened them with his gun and fiendishly rocked the damaged stagecoach.

Sirrus looked as if he'd like to help the ladies escape from this hell-hole but he knew Bart wouldn't agree and that he'd as likely kill them. He knew they had the oriental man with them, so they'd get help from him.

Soames Ho wanted to get out the coach but Tootsie held on to his arm.

'Don't try any heroics, Mr Ho,' she said. 'What we gals gonna do if they kill you too?'

Soames Ho nodded. He'd bide his time. The man who'd rocked the stagecoach had done him a favour. As he'd stumbled he touched the knife, his ivory-handled one, which he'd slipped into his boot. Although he'd locked up his guns, he'd not parted with a present from his grandfather.

When the gals, quieter now, but mesmerized by the gunmen, turned their attention from him, he climbed out of the stagecoach and slipped away.

Soames Ho was determined that the men would

pay for what they'd done this day. They were halfway up the hill. Bart Ford's voice could be heard as he cussed Sirrus Warman like it was his fault the box got caught up in obstacles along the way.

Soames Ho slid across the ground, his belly low, like a snake. In his hand he held the knife like a viper's tongue.

Bart Ford didn't feel the cut of the knife across his neck. Soames Ho sliced deep. The jugular spurted out dark red blood and left a pattern like a cobweb across the ground.

Sirrus Warman, too late it turned out, saw the oriental man wield his knife. He saw a glazed look film over Bart Ford's eyes, and then a sigh told Sirrus the man wouldn't see anything else again.

Soames Ho pushed Bart's body aside and moved fast to get to Sirrus Warman but he wasn't quick enough and a fist hit out viciously and caught him on the bridge of his nose. He yelped in pain before he slashed out at Sirrus. He knew it had struck home for the outlaw pulled back wounded, but it did him no good. Soames Ho lost his foothold and tumbled back down the slope and towards the stagecoach.

Sirrus Warman couldn't believe his good fortune, and hauled the box up the last few feet. At the top, past the trees, he looked down at the scene of carnage he'd left behind.

He noticed one of the women passengers being helped out of the stagecoach by the man who'd attacked him. The woman's bright magenta-coloured silk dress shimmered as it caught the sun. Then the man shielded his eyes with his hand as he scanned the horizon above Savage Pass. For a moment their eyes met and the man shook his fist in Sirrus's direction. Joaquin Mateo or Bart Ford would've shot him down just for the fun of it. Sirrus Warman had no more taste left for that. He saw the man turn away to help his other companions.

Black buzzards began to circle overhead. They didn't waste time. Soon bones would be picked clean and then left to dry out under the sun.

After he tied a strip of cloth, ripped from the tail of his shirt, around his arm, Sirrus Warman strapped the heavy box onto the saddle of Joaquin Mateo's horse. Before he mounted his own horse he pulled on his jacket to keep any midges away from the wound. Given the chance they liked to feast on a bit of blood.

He slapped the rump of Bart Ford's mare and it galloped away. He didn't want to be slowed down by a string of horses.

He determined to bury the dang gold where no one else would find it. Perhaps later he'd return and some good would come of all this. Although the only

37

thing he could ever associate it with was bad luck.

It seemed to him that the box of gold had caused all this trouble and he'd take it away and hide it.

It was cursed.

CHAPTER SIX

In the shanks of the evening Sirrus Warman became aware that a pair of eyes watched him. Whoever it was must be secreted behind the small bushes, because when he tried, surreptitiously, to see who was there, the person was completely hidden from view. The eyes burned into his back like an unskilled dentist trying out his drill and piercing the roots of a tooth.

Sirrus didn't turn right round, or make out that he knew he was being observed as he went about his business. He'd find the watcher soon enough. He tried to act natural as he surveyed the area and stood and scratched at his now wet armpits. The sun might be going down but the still warm air and the exertion of his task caused sweat to pour from him. He slapped away a pesky fly that buzzed around him, attracted perhaps by blood that still oozed from the cut to his arm.

Sirrus had ended up God knows where in this countryside. After he had left the scene of the stagecoach robbery, he'd headed west, followed the sun and travelled towards the foothills of the Sierra Nevada. The great mountains seemed to beckon him towards them and he followed their call. He wanted to find a place to bury the box of gold. He wanted rid of it before it did any more damage. Now he took his spade, nicknamed his miner's banjo, the only thing he'd ever played a tune with, and started to dig.

In his mind it wasn't Joaquin Mateo or Bart Ford who'd killed the two men. It wasn't he, Sirrus, who'd pushed his partner over the edge of Savage Pass, and left the passengers, at least the women passengers, and ignored their screams for help. No, the gold had caused all the trouble.

The sun had borne down on him all afternoon and his thoughts had ceased to be straight. He'd jumbled the facts until he put the blame for events on the very thing he'd coveted.

And now, as he stooped over the hole he'd started to dig, it seemed to him that his effort to put everything to rights by burying the bad luck could be thwarted. He cursed inwardly. Although he'd stumbled into the area, he'd looked for quite a while to find this particular spot. The place, just inside the neck of a cave, where the ground was soft, looked as if it had been used by a grizzly bear in winter for its hibernation. The floor, strewn with stripped carcases and bones sucked white, bore witness to a feast. Sure seemed a big one, Sirrus thought, and judged by the amount of food waste, the bear could be about four hundred pounds. Anyone who stumbled across this place might find themselves in the belly of the cave's occupant. This suited him fine. It would also give him time to decide what to do with the gold; maybe he'd retrieve the strongbox next summer when the bad luck had gone, he mused.

All this time, as he dug, he felt the eyes never left him and he visualized holes right in the back of the buffalo skin coat he wore. Its fringes swished to and fro as he moved rhythmically back and forth. He decided to increase the hole in the ground until it was large enough to place a body as well as a box in it. Anyone who knew his secret best be buried alongside it, he thought.

Light Weaver, a young Indian, had left her camp early that morning. Her mother, too busy and distracted by chores, hadn't noticed her slip away. Her father never concerned himself with what the women in the camp did and left them to their own devices. Only her elder brother commented about her intended absence, and said that it could be unsafe to go out alone.

'Light Weaver has no enemies, my brother,' she laughed.

She saw the frown on his face but was gone before he had time to say anything else. She carried with her a cake, made mainly of acorns, but she'd find some berries to eat with it and fresh water to drink from a stream. Most of their food, fuel and clothes came from the earth, although a few worked on the ranches in the valley. Light Weaver wore the skin of a mule deer, two pieces front and back held together with plant twine and in the distance, with her pale brown skin, she might be mistaken for a small graceful doe.

She'd come out today to find some special plants to weave into her baskets. She was a good basket weaver. Light Weaver looked for something different to add to the fern roots, white willow twigs and brown marsh grass roots that she often used to weave. She'd noticed a lovely lupin flower near the south Yuba River and she wanted that. However somehow she'd become sidetracked and trailed after some red and yellow alpine lilies. She wanted to make some special baskets, to save for the day she'd be united with an Indian brave of her family's choice, because this year she would be past fourteen summers and it was almost time.

Now she found herself on the western slopes of the Sierra and into the path of the white man. When Light Weaver came across the man who dug at the mouth of the bear's cave she didn't realize this would be her last summer.

Sirrus Warman, after a while, decided he was mistaken about being watched by someone who coveted the gold. He'd got the heebie-jeebies about everything today. It was probably only a deer, perhaps a young one, which got separated from the herd and now lost and frightened, it lingered hidden behind some shrubbery. No one else would be around in the Sierra foothills. It surely was a beautiful place but isolated and off the beaten track where he'd found the perfect spot to stow his gold.

In fact, he had decided, when he'd thought about it earlier, he wasn't far from his brother's ranch just outside of Marysville, maybe a half-day's ride away. He hadn't been there for a few months. Sirrus stood and tugged at his yellow, ragged moustache; no, hell, it dawned on him it must be over a year since he had set foot on the Warman's Longhorn Ranch. He and his brother hadn't seen eye to eye for a while. Emmett Warman had hit gold and then bought a ranch. Where others had gambled their gold away, Emmett had invested and prospered.

He'd had little time for a brother who couldn't or

43

wouldn't work as hard as he had done. Sirrus knew that because the last time he'd seen Emmett his brother had darn well told him. Emmett wasn't afraid to speak plain words.

Sirrus decided that if he called into the ranch then he'd better go with a small gift at least. It would earn him some respect if he could lay some game on his brother's table.

He took another break, wiped his brow with the back of his hand and as he rested his foot on his old miner's banjo he'd pushed into the ground, he relaxed. He stretched his back and took the strain from his a spine that ached. His arm throbbed and he decided to call it a day. The hole was more than deep enough. All the time he moved slowly. He didn't want to startle the deer in the bush. No sudden movements or he knew he could say goodbye to the succulent meat. His gun rested by the wall of the cave near his shotgun and Sirrus reached out, picked it up and checked the bullets in the barrel, all with a smooth silent action. Sirrus was sure where the deer waited and watched ever since he'd arrived and he turned towards it.

In an almost single action he'd aimed and fired. He heard a cry that was strangely human as the slugs hit their target. He'd got the jackpot, he thought as he walked over towards the kill.

The young Indian girl had no chance to bolt and avoid the shotgun. She should have gone long ago but her curiosity had held her. Intrigued to find out why the white man was at the mouth of the bear's cave, Light Weaver didn't see the danger. She felt a sharp pain and looked down to see her clothing spattered with red. Too late, it registered on her that she'd been shot, as she fell to the ground.

Sirrus reached the spot at the same time as the life ebbed away from the girl.

'God dang!' he cried.

Too late, it occured to him he ought to have made sure what he fired at. The damage was done. He didn't have to touch her to know she was dead meat. Quickly he looked around to make sure there were no others about. Last thing he wanted was a bunch of Indians out to string him up. If that's all they did, because Sirrus shivered as he recalled all the stories he'd heard of how Indians tortured their captives. It was all with no provocation, it was just because white men had come on to what they called 'their land'. Place was big enough for everybody, Sirrus Warman thought. But that wasn't the problem now. He'd certainly given them a reason to be angry and what would they do if they had a reason?

He knew he had to get out of there fast. The night had finally drawn in to pitch black as he stood there and dithered. He'd started to shake in his boots so much that he cursed himself.

'No use acting like a long-tailed cat in a room full of rocking chairs.'

Finally, when the clouds cleared and the light of the full white moon illuminated the scene, Sirrus used the light to guide him. He picked up the girl, carried her across to the hole he'd dug in the cave and placed her side by side with the gold.

Somewhere a wolf howled and soon all its other canine friends joined in. Sirrus shivered again as he shovelled the dirt back into the hole and then crossed himself as if to ward off any evil spirits that might lurk around the place. The cave started to look like a black pit and in his fanciful imaginings he saw it as a gateway to hell. He wanted to throw the stones over the body and strongbox in his haste to be gone but he forced himself to take care over the task. This ought to remain a secret forever. Sirrus then walked back to the place he'd left his horse to graze without once taking a look back at that awful place.

Although Sirrus had nothing to offer, he decided there was no choice but to go to his brother's ranch and ask if he could stay there awhile. But if Sirrus thought he was going to have an easy journey he was mistaken.

CHAPTER SEVEN

The women and the man knew they had to move from the stagecoach. Although one outlaw lay dead and the other had tumbled into the ravine the area was a mighty inhospitable place at night-time when the temperature would drop with the setting sun.

Soames Ho's instinct was to follow the last outlaw and retrieve the gold but he had to turn back with the three women who now turned to him for help. They had to make their way towards a town, near Marysville, which they'd passed through a few hours before. It was a safe port of call for all of them.

Soames Ho fashioned a makeshift stretcher for Mrs Ryder with blankets and thin strong branches. She'd been wounded by the bullet Joaquin Mateo aimed at her when she'd been foolish enough to stick her head out of the coach. She'd bled profusely at first, enough to stain her light-brown woollen bloomer-suit with dark red patches, but the saloon gals ripped up petticoats and bound her well enough to stop the bleeding.

Tootsie and Mae gamely held onto the two corners of one end of the stretcher and he took the other end and they marched onwards with Mrs Ryder nestled inside it. Soames Ho knew he would have to come back later. But this time he'd be armed with guns. He hadn't been ready to challenge three men armed with pistols and shotguns with women around. One of them had already been harmed by the varmints who'd stolen the green strongbox of gold and he hadn't been able to risk the other women. They, too, could've been hurt, or worse, as well.

Inside he felt angry at the Pinkerton agent. The company had underplayed the dangers of this trip. They'd said he was merely to escort the gold to the bank and make sure it was signed over. They'd said nothing about the chances of a robbery. Although these thoughts floated through his mind, it was too late because he ought to have taken it into account and perhaps the last few weeks had taken something out of him. But on the outside, he kept his aura of inscrutability, and calmed the ladies' hysteria.

The marshal in Marysville hadn't expected to see

the strange young man again. After all, he'd said he had finished with everything that reminded him about the terrible things that had happened to his kin.

'Got bad news to report in,' Soames Ho said.

He'd left the ladies as soon as they'd been booked into a hotel, then he rode straight back to Marysville to relay the information to the marshal. A few men were despatched to get the bodies of Dan Buckon and Miles Tay and another group, made up of townswomen and Doc Barrington, went to tend the females, back at the hotel in the nearby town.

When the news of the robbery got out it was received with anger.

'Damn well trusted them with my gold and where's it all gone?' said one miner.

'I might as well have buried it. That-a-ways I'd have a good idea where it was,' said another.

There was talk of a lynching, but it soon fizzled out when they found there was no one to lynch. Although the marshal had to calm things down when a gang of men, well saturated with whiskey came over to the law office and demanded to know how come the oriental managed to escape to tell the tale. When the oriental man stepped onto the porch behind marshal they stopped baying for his blood. His tall, imposing, wiry frame and mean expression

49

commanded respect.

'I'm going to look for the men. And I swear I'll bring the gold back here.'

Somehow his dark hooded eyes didn't allow for any argument. The gang dispersed.

'How you gonna do that?' the marshal asked. They were alone again. 'You ain't no law man.'

They sat together in the marshal's office and the marshal pulled a cork out the bottle of whiskey and poured them both a glass each.

'Ain't thought that out yet,' he answered. He ignored the marshal's remark about him not being a law man. 'But I don't like being made a fool of.'

Soames Ho couldn't locate the whereabouts of the Pinkerton agent who'd hired him and when he telegraphed Allan Pinkerton at the head office in Chicago he got a surprise. Lode Pinkerton had no connection with the agency. The Pinkerton Agency officially hired Soames Ho on the spot. They wanted him to find out what had happened and to bring the outlaws to justice.

He gave the marshal the news.

'Looks like you're all official now, Soames Ho,' he agreed.

Luke Yale, alias Lode Pinkerton, scurried away from Marysville a few hours after the stagecoach had left town. Luke Yale travelled from town to town to con fools out of their money. And it never failed to surprise him just how many fools there were in this world. When he hit on the idea of a robbery on a stagecoach full of gold, and pretended to be Pinkerton's cousin, no one had questioned the deception. So after he'd got rid of Joe Ferns by adding enough poisonous mushrooms to that pork stew to make him sick, he was able to substitute a young kid who'd probably spend all his bullets shooting at shadows. His judgement wasn't questioned. The company always sent an agent, as well as a driver and shotgun rider, with the coach. It would've looked odd for him to volunteer so he'd asked the oriental guy. It was a perfect choice; a man so sick of violence that he never even carried a gun with him.

That was until the peaceful man rode back into town, and vowed to find those who'd robbed the stagecoach.

Soames Ho took up his guns again. He had thought he'd left all that behind when he'd dealt with those rogues that'd killed his family. Now it seemed to him that there still was a need to police the West, and make it a better place for people to live. He tooled up with a couple of .44 Peacemakers in his belt and

51

a .22 derringer in his top waistcoat pocket. At his side, strapped to his horse's saddle, was his favourite, a Henry .44 repeater rifle.

He started to ask a few questions around Yuba County. He spent time getting to know everyone. Even the Indians were his friends. He frequently negotiated in disputes between them and the white settlers. In turn they respected the man they called Yellow Hide.

And three names had frequently cropped up.

The names were Joaquin Mateo, Sirrus Warman and Bart Ford. He knew the man he'd killed was Bart Ford so he got crossed off his list; but he vowed he'd find the other two, and the *hombre* with the fictitious name. It might take some time. But time didn't trouble him.

He had all the time in the world.

CHAPTER EIGHT

Back in Savage Pass, after the passengers left, someone else moved.

Joaquin Mateo, although he'd lost consciousness after his fall, slowly began to stir. He opened his eyes. His head throbbed. The last thing he could remember were some women who screamed fit to bust. Then the memories flooded back. And they hurt more than the lump on his head.

'Curse that scallawag,' he cried. He gritted his teeth. 'I must've been plumb weak north of my ears to take him on this job with me. And God knows what's happened to Bart.'

He tried to crawl to his knees. Pain went through him like a million hot needles and he collapsed down in a heap.

'I shouldn't have listened to that critter Luke Yale,

who told me about the gold.'

He thumped the ground with his fist then winced as he hit the solid rock beneath him with the damaged hand. He remembered that damn horse had kicked out and caught him. *Thank goodness I practiced using my gun with both hands*, he thought.

Slowly he rolled over to his side and started to get to his feet. This time he was more successful but he still wobbled about like he was as drunk as a fiddler's clerk and sat down again. Joaquin felt in his waistcoat pocket for his flask.

'A little bit of gut warmer will make me well,' he said.

He stretched his neck and felt the fiery liquid slip down his throat. Apart from the twisted fingers and a few aches, lumps and bruises he had got off lightly. He struggled to rip one of the bands, tied over the bottom of his pants, to keep them tight to his leg. Then he'd have something to bind his hand and support the swollen fingers; at least he'd stand a chance in a fight. He moved his fingers to check he hadn't broken the bones although it damn sure hurt, then he bound them tight. At last he felt ready to move off. He vowed he'd find that son of a bitch, Sirrus Warman, if it was the last thing he did. And he'd find out why Bart Ford hadn't come to his aid. Out loud he promised himself that he'd take all the gold.

'Warman, or Ford, ain't gonna have any of it, nor that critter, Luke Yale, who wanted a cut for the information supplied.'

He almost laughed at the thought of the fool expecting a reward for the information he'd given to him, Joaquin Mateo, to rob the stagecoach.

But laughter wasn't in his nature and he cursed instead.

He edged his way along the crevice where he'd fallen and when he was out of sight of the man and women who might still be in the stagecoach, he crawled up the side, holding onto rocks and bushes with his good hand to give him anchorage until he found the path again.

To follow a trail held no difficulty for Joaquin Mateo. He'd spent his youth on the land. He knew the desert so well he ought to have given all the lizards pet names, and the mountain trails were like the veins on the back of his grizzled and scarred hands. He knew the names of trees, flowers, butterflies and birds. If he'd made different choices he could've done something better with his life.

But he'd chosen to walk hand in hand with the devil. And he promised himself he'd get some enjoyment when he caught up with Sirrus Warman, the varmint who'd cast him over the edge of Savage Pass, and Bart Ford who'd deserted him.

What was going to prove difficult was to find a horse.

Eventually he reached the top where they'd tethered their horses. Joaquin Matco found that they were gone. It was to be expected, he knew, but it still hit hard when he discovered it as a fact. He looked down Savage Pass again. There were four horses there still strapped to the stagecoach. He'd have to take one. He still had one of his Peacemakers tucked in his belt and he took out his gun ready in case anyone decided to play at being brave and attack him.

As he moved down he came across Bart Ford's body.

'Fool,' muttered Joaquin.

He pushed him to one side, even more wary now, because he decided he'd underestimated Sirrus Warman. It seemed to him that Warman wanted all the gold for himself and would go to any length to get it.

In fact it was all quiet when he got down to the stagecoach. He could only think they'd decided to head back whence they came. It suited him. He didn't want to shoot them, he thought, because he couldn't afford to waste the bullets.

He picked up the shotgun rider's gun, still loaded, from the side of his body. Not a nice sight. The big black flies had started to buzz round looking for sweet meat to lay their eggs in. They'd have to fight it out with the buzzards soon; and any big cats on the lookout for an easy meal. Joaquin scanned the place to make sure none were here already. He didn't want to add himself to the menu. He pulled free the harness that trapped the four horses and led out the bigger lead horse. He grabbed at its mane as it tried to rear up.

'Quiet. You bested me once with those hoofs of yours, but you'll learn I'm your master now.' he hissed.

Joaquin Mateo pulled at the bit between its teeth and heard it whinny as the metal dug into its soft flesh. Then he jumped up onto its back, held on tight to its head harness and pressed his thighs together to secure himself on its back. The horse calmed down. Joaquin knew about horseflesh. He knew how to control the beast. He dug his spurs into its side and together they rode out of Savage Pass.

CHAPTER NINE

Sirrus Warman, unaware of the danger that followed him, slumped forward in his saddle as he rode his mare. He'd unsaddled Joaquin's horse after he'd led her some miles away and left her to graze. He knew he couldn't turn up at his brother's place with another man's horse. The unwritten code of the West was that you never took a man's horse. So if he did, Emmett wouldn't be satisfied until he had a few answers.

Sirrus knew he'd not be welcome at Warman's Longhorn Range if he told the truth about what he'd been up to. He'd best keep that to himself, he decided. In fact, he knew he'd have to keep it close to his chest forever. Sirrus moved as slow as a crippled turtle but he couldn't find it him to hurry onwards. Today had been a nightmare but the only thing was, he wouldn't be waking up from it. Tomorrow would bring the same set of dreams and they stunk higher than a mildewed blanket after it had been rid on a sore back horse three hundred miles in August. And that was bad.

His horse plodded onwards as it carried its load, as if it knew its way home. Had Sirrus been faster it would have been better for him. As it was, Joaquin Mateo wasn't too far behind him and by the end of the day, he was upon him. Although Sirrus almost had his brother's ranch in his sights it might as well been a hundred miles away.

'Step down, *amigo*.' The familiar voice brought Sirrus to his senses.

He'd been deep in his thoughts and had forgotten the reality of the situation. Joaquin Mateo, alive and well, a shotgun pointed square at Sirrus Warman's head, stood in front of him. Joaquin wasn't about to take any chances with a damaged hand. He managed to hold the gun firmly enough so he could blow his one-time partner to smithereens.

Sirrus, shocked at the sight of Joaquin Mateo, stopped his horse in its tracks.

'I thought you—'

The other man finished the sentence for him.

'Oh yes. *amigo*, you thought I was dead like Bart Ford. Well, have I got some bad news. And it's going to disappoint you. I'm very much alive. You don't look so good though.'

For Joaquin Mateo this was a long speech. He chewed on his tobacco wad and then spat out some yellow juice. He was in no hurry. He had plenty of time. All the time he kept his eye on the man on the horse. One untoward move from Sirrus Warman and he'd punch him full of holes. But Joaquin Mateo didn't want that to happen, yet.

'I didn't kill Bart Ford,' Sirrus protested. 'The feller from the stagecoach crept up on us. . . .'

Joaquin was in no mood to listen to silly stories and told Sirrus Warman to shut up and get down from his horse.

Faced with a shotgun aimed at his chest Sirrus reluctantly obeyed Joaquin Mateo's command. He couldn't do anything else. But an inner sense of preservation took control. Sirrus knew that once he stood in front of Joaquin Mateo he was a dead man. Or put another way, a man who'd die slowly. He'd seen Joaquin in action too many times to think that he would let him off that lightly.

In fact, Sirrus knew he'd been a fool to become involved with the man. It was the thought of easy money that had lured him in. As Sirrus slid down the side of his horse, he pulled the shot gun out of its holster by the saddle.

Foolishly, Joaquin Mateo hadn't bothered to strip him of guns. The events of the past few days must have affected his brain, Sirrus thought. He fired. He didn't bother to take aim. He knew if he could get the slugs to go in the right general direction, then he'd at least wound the man and stand a chance against him.

Joaquin Mateo saw Sirrus stumble from his horse. Before his mind focused on the fact that Sirrus hadn't fallen off, and got his wits about him to pull the trigger of his own gun, his uninjured lower left arm had been blown into a mash of flesh and splintered bone by the shot gun. For a split second he stood, dumbstruck, to the spot. He knew then he'd missed his chance to kill Sirrus Warman and he'd paid a heavy price. A scream of rage and pain emerged from his mouth as he fell, bleeding, to the ground.

Joaquin Mateo's anger stopped him from a slide into unconsciousness. He looked at the mess that was his arm and screamed curses at the man who'd left him out here to die. His own horse, the one he'd recovered on his journey to find Sirrus Warman, had bolted. He wished now he hadn't shot the other horse. The thing had damaged his hand with its hoof and he'd delighted in killing it once he'd finished with it. Trouble was, he'd done it a little too soon. He knew that had he tied the two horses together they'd

61

have slowed down after their initial flight. Now he'd nothing to carry him to find help.

Sirrus Warman got back on his horse. 'Gee up!' he shouted at the startled animal. The beast didn't take much to goad it into action. It took off as if all the devils from hell were after it. And, if Joaquin Mateo's screams of anger and pain were to be believed, then it was he who'd sent them after the horse and rider.

Sirrus Warman hadn't got off without a payback from Joaquin Mateo. Slow as the other man had been, he'd managed to fire his gun as Sirrus took him down. Sirrus's side was full of lead and he wondered if he'd make it to his brother's place at all.

For a while, people just paused from their work and stared at a horse and rider that made their way, haphazardly across the grasslands towards the ranch. Then someone galloped to Warman's Longhorn Ranch to forewarn Emmett that he had a visitor. Meanwhile Sirrus Warman's horse plodded onwards. The man's head hung forward, his eyelids drooped down along with his yellow moustache and he stayed on the saddle only because he'd wound the reins round his wrists and bound them to the neck of his saddle.

Emmett Warman knew a man was travelling towards the ranch before his daughter ran out shrieking the news.

'Pa, Pa. It's Uncle Sirrus.'

Grace Warman, a fourteen-year-old girl, with red-blonde hair and willow-green eyes inherited from her mother, emerged from the house. Her brown freckled face was the result of life on a California ranch. She had seen Sirrus as she looked out the small window above the kitchen sink. She ran out and called to her pa when she recognized the rider of the horse. She danced up and down as she watched her favourite, albeit a scarcely-seen uncle, ride up the Warman's Longhorn Ranch path. Grace rubbed her soapy hands on the sides of the white homespun cotton apron which covered her split-skirt riding dress.

'I can see,' Emmett Warman admonished his daughter. 'And don't crowd him. He sure looks like he's had a long hard ride.'

Emmett sighed inwardly at the sight of his younger brother. He and Sirrus had come out West together well over fifteen years ago. Whilst he'd struck gold, his brother had just struck bad luck, or so he said. Emmett had invested his gold whilst Sirrus, refusing to share the gold his brother had found, had carried on searching. But all Sirrus had found were problems which, unfortunately, he'd always brought back to Emmett's door. Sirrus's independence had cost him dear, Emmett thought.

'Is he all right, Pa?'

Her pa heard the horror in his daughter's voice and looked at the weary man on the horse and saw the blood-stained shirt he wore.

'Al,' he shouted. 'Come and help me with this man.'

Al Brown, the foreman at Warman's Longhorn Ranch, stopped his work and ran across to help his boss. 'It looks like my brother has been shot. Send someone to get Doc Barrington,' Emmett said. 'Grace, don't you stand there like a ninny. Go and get a pallet ready and some bandages.'

Grace Warman didn't need to be told twice, the heels of her brown, laced boots turned in flight as she ran into the house to do as her pa bid.

Emmett and Al set Sirrus on the bed she'd pulled out in a corner of their living quarters, and quickly took his coat off so they could see where he had been wounded.

'Someone has taken a piece out of his side,' Al commented.

A gasp came from Grace, who stood near to the two men, as the extent of the damage to Sirrus became revealed.

'Get out the way, girl, if you can't stand the sight of a bit of blood,' Emmett said gruffly to his daughter.

'I'm fine, Pa.'

He looked at the now white-faced girl.

'Go make us all some coffee.'

The injury wasn't easy for him to deal with, let alone for a young girl. They bound Sirrus's wound up and when the doc came, he said he couldn't do much more. Doc Barrington added gunpowder and flour to the dressing and suggested they change it every day. He also gave them a potion of morphine for whenever Sirrus cried out in pain.

'And don't forget to pray,' he added.

Grace became Sirrus's nurse. She wiped his brow and put a cloth dipped in water to stop his lips drying out. He couldn't swallow any food, and the only thing which gave him relief was the doc's potion. But after a few days, Sirrus's colour returned and he ate a few spoonfuls of the soup Grace made. Doc Barrington, pleased with the condition of his wound, told them to continue with the same treatment. The gun had perforated the side but no lead had lodged in his body.

'Looks like you're a lucky man,' the doc observed.

That same night Sirrus started burning up and complained that his belly gave him pains.

'You must've put something bad in that stew,' Emmett joked but one look at Grace, and then at Sirrus, he regretted his words. 'I'll get the doc back,' he said.

'Sorry,' said the doc, as he examined Sirrus's tender bloated abdomen, 'looks like he's more damaged inside than we thought.'

He prescribed sassafras tea for the fever and some more morphine for the pain. He shook his head at Emmett as he left. They both knew nothing more could be done. That didn't persuade Grace to leave her Uncle Sirrus and go to bed. As young as she was, Grace was determined to stay. Emmett let her have her way. Her uncle would die soon and death was a fact of life that Grace knew all about. Her own mother had caught a fever and died two years back. Grace had sat and held her mother's hand until she passed away.

In the middle of that very same night, Sirrus opened his eyes and spoke to Grace.

'Can you write?' he asked.

Grace pulled herself up straight in her chair about to protest that Ma had taught her to read, write and add up numbers and made her practise almost up until she'd died. And she still practised. But the look on her Uncle Sirrus's face made her bite her tongue. He was too ill to want to know that.

'I want you to write a letter. And get some paper for me to draw a map.'

The funeral took place a few days later. Grace reckoned that his death had been hastened by a visit from a man who said he was a Pinkerton agent. The man had nigh on tried to murder her Uncle, and Pa had thrown him out. It had been a bad couple of weeks. She hid the letter underneath the wool mattress on her trundle bed. Uncle Sirrus told her it was their secret. She'd have to wait until Pa took her to town before she could find someone who would, on their journey east, carry it to its Midwest address.

Not that Emmett Warman was in the mood to go into town. Before winter he'd need everyone out to find stray cattle. Then the stock would be counted, branded and fattened up before were sent on the cattle drive to the markets in the North. He had practically no hands to do the work on the ranch because all the Indian workers had disappeared.

CHAPTER TEN

Luke Yale had run out of town before the news of the robbery got back to Marysville. He'd been determined to leave before the anger of the miners let rip, and they started to hunt someone down to hang. And if they discovered that Luke wasn't who he said he was, then he'd be swinging on a tree from a Californian collar before the day was over.

When he arrived at Savage Pass there was nothing there but a broken stagecoach and dead bodies. And, of course, plenty of buzzards, who flapped their heavy wings above the scene. He shuddered at the birds that waited for the blowflies to soften the corpses before they alighted. Then they'd be ready to pluck at the flesh with their large hooked beaks.

Joaquin Mateo and Sirrus Warman had already left the scene of carnage. Bart Ford hadn't been so lucky.

Luke couldn't find any passengers from the stagecoach, not that he looked too far inside the vehicle. He'd already aired his paunch once, and he didn't want to search for anything else to upset it, he'd decided. He wondered briefly about the young man Soames Ho, and then pushed the thought away. No doubt he'd hightailed it back to town because he'd no stomach for a fight.

Luke scratched at the stubble on his face. His hair was shiny black straight from a bottle, but he couldn't disguise the natural grey stuff that sprouted from his chin. These past couple of days had caught him short and his true self poked through. His bloodshot eyes and lined face made him look as ugly as the hindquarters of bad luck.

In his profession he knew he couldn't afford to look rough. He considered himself a debonair type of man. Even in this savage place he buttoned his jacket over his large paunch and checked to make sure he hadn't marked his suit. He wiped the sweat from his brow with an off-white handkerchief and then pushed it back into the pocket of his wrinkled pants.

As a con man he never knew when a rich widow-woman, young or old, would look for comfort in his arms. Or sometimes he'd pass himself off as a financial expert with advice about how to invest other people's money.

The world was full of fools.

But this was the first time he'd been involved with a robbery, and from the way it had gone so far, it would be the last.

Luke Yale followed the trail that his comrades in crime had taken. More by accident than design, he watched in alarm the fight between Joaquin Mateo and Sirrus Warman, and when he assumed the half-breed Mexican was dead, he hung around for a while wondering what to do. Just as he decided he'd best go after Sirrus Warman, he saw a group of Indians drag Joaquin away.

He kept his presence a secret. He reckoned he'd soon smell the aroma of burning flesh if there was any life left in the body of Joaquin. He'd heard that the red man had lost a lot of their initial respect and fear of the white man. It seemed that after the loss of their lands to the newcomers and the battles that ensued, there were nasty rumours about the treatment meted out by the Indians in return. He backed away from the mêlée; he, a city guy at heart, felt out of his depth in the wild blue yonder.

When it became quiet again, Luke wandered back to the spot where he'd last seen Joaquin Mateo and the Indians. Apart from a patch of dark sticky stuff he noticed under his feet on the grassy ground, there was nothing to indicate that anyone had been there at all. Only a metallic smell, when he touched it with his fingers, assured him it was blood.

'Nothing I can do here,' he muttered.

And as he didn't want to risk his own blood to be added to the spot should the Indians come back, Luke Yale followed in the direction Sirrus Warman had taken less than an hour earlier.

When he approached Warman's Longhorn Ranch, he figured it was the only place that Sirrus Warman could've headed. Luke Yale wanted to talk to Sirrus but the place was thronged with cowmen who probably wouldn't bat an eye if they had to take out an intruder. He waited for a few days, watched folk come and go. At last he decided he couldn't take the chance that they'd become aware of the stranger who hung around the ranch uninvited. Those with legitimate reasons went up to the front door. Anyone else could be mistaken for a cattle rustler.

Also Luke knew that he had to find out what had happened to the gold.

'What's your business, friend?'

A tall sturdy-looking man, Luke took to be the foreman, approached him. Luke Yale nodded his head in greeting but kept his hands on the reins of his horse just to show the feller he wasn't going to go for a gun. He didn't want to appear unfriendly.

'Name's Lode Pinkerton,' Luke said. 'Need to speak to Sirrus Warman. I hear he's visiting here.'

Luke decided that his false name would hold him in good stead here. This place was way too far out to pick up news fast.

'Wait here.'

Luke sat and waited. He thought it wise to do as he was told and he had nowhere else to go at the moment. The other ranch hands worked quietly around him, but he sensed that on a word from the big man he'd be trussed up like one of the steers ready for the branding iron.

'I'm Emmett Warman,' the man said. 'It seems you've got mighty fine hearing.'

Luke Yale ignored the note of sarcasm.

'So what you want with my brother?'

Luke looked down on a thin wiry man. He could see Sirrus around the eyes, deep-set with dark-brown pupils but these seemed to bore into a man's soul. Luke mentally shook himself. The events of the day were making him fanciful.

'I'm Lode Pinkerton,' he repeated, 'from the Pinkerton Detective Agency. I employed Sirrus Warman to do a job for me.'

Luke decided that was the nearest explanation. Sirrus's brother sneered at him.

'Well, hell, that's the first time I've heard work and

Sirrus in the same sentence. You sure you got the right man?'

Luke, surprised at the bitterness in the man's voice, noticed blood stains on the brother's shirt. Emmett caught the direction of his gaze.

'Sirrus is none too good. He's taken a bullet or two in his side,' he said.

'I need to speak to him,' Luke pleaded.

He expected to be refused the request then Emmett Warman shrugged his shoulders.

'You'll get nothing outta him. But satisfy yourself.'

Luke Yale got down from the horse and followed Emmett inside while one of the ranch hands looked after his horse. In the house Luke saw Sirrus lying on a truckle bed, with a young girl by his side. She looked up as she wiped Sirrus's brow.

'How is he?' Luke asked.

'This man wants to talk to your uncle.'

'He's not too good.'

Luke could hear the protest in her voice and her reluctance to move when her father ordered her to leave them alone. Luke Yale waited for the place to empty. The look of concern slipped from his face and he shook the semi-conscious man violently.

'Sirrus, Sirrus,' he hissed into the man's ear, 'what on earth happened to the gold?'

'What. . . ?' Sirrus moved into a level of

consciousness that allowed an understanding of what was happening around him. 'What do you want?'

'The gold.' Luke kept his voice low. But the note of menace still held. 'What did you do with it?'

Sirrus's mouth pulled into a grotesque parody of a grin and spittle dribbled out. Luke shook him again. He knew he had to get an answer before he croaked but there'd be little time before the girl came back in. She'd only gone because of her pa's orders but he guessed she'd be back, order or no order to stay away.

'I ain't got it,' Sirrus said. His eyes moved wildly in their sockets so at times only the whites were visible. 'Joaquin Mateo and Bart Ford have got the gold.'

'You're a liar.' Luke Yale grabbed hold of Sirrus Warman's shoulders and pulled him to sitting position. 'I know you killed Bart Ford. I saw the Indians take Joaquin. He's probably bubbling in a stew in some Indian tepee. Tell me what happened . . . or I'll kill you.'

Luke had pulled a derringer from his pocket; it was a neat little friend that came to his aid on occasions. This could be one of them. The little gun pressed against Sirrus's forehead so hard it left an impression there. Sirrus's face twisted into an unnatural distortion of a smile.

'Kill me then . . . it'll save the Lord the effort. . . .'

74

The other man turned purple with rage. The whole thing had been a farce from beginning to end. However the amount of gold on the stagecoach wasn't to be sneered at. He'd told Joaquin Mateo, Sirrus Warman and Bart Ford about it and he ought to have his share. As he looked at the state of Sirrus, and imaged the fate of Joaquin, and recalled the image of Bart Ford, then as far as he was concerned the gold ought to be his now. Soon he would be the only one left and when that happened, no one would be able to tell him where the gold had gone. He pocketed the derringer. Then he shook Sirrus again until the man's head flopped and the blood from the wound seeped through his nightshirt.

Eventually Luke Yale let him go and Sirrus fell back onto the bed. This would get him nowhere, he decided.

'Sirrus,' he pleaded, 'if you tell me where the gold is, I'll make sure your niece has some of the money.'

Sirrus's eyes opened again and the lips curled into a sneer. 'Like hell you will. . . .'

Luke Yale saw red. He grabbed hold of Sirrus's shirt and brought him face to face, eyeball to eyeball, and shouted at him.

'You bastard. You don't need the money. Give it to me.'

His fists balled up and smacked the injured man in

75

the face. He was so hell-bent on getting the information from him he didn't notice Grace Warman come back into the room.

'Get off him,' she screamed.

At the sound of raised voices, the door smashed open so forcefully it almost zinged off its hinges. Al Brown led a trio of Emmett's ranch hands into the room. They pulled Luke Yale off the sick man and out the door so fast he thought he'd meet up with himself riding out of town a few days ago. Although a big man, his feet barely touched the ground.

'Don't you come back here again,' Emmett Warman shouted out as Luke Yale was thrown over his horse and ordered off the ranch.

'You come back here and you'll be on a sickbed yourself.'

Luke didn't need to be told twice. He was out of sight as soon as he could pull himself upright on his saddle and ride out of Warman's Longhorn Ranch.

But he didn't go far. He found a place to nestle in the hills and wait. Meanly fortified by an occasional rabbit too stupid to realize that man wasn't his best friend, a bottle of whiskey and a plenty of plugs of tobacco, he kept watch on the ranch. When, during the beginning of the second week, at the point he was about to call it quits, he saw a coffin and all the trimmings of a funeral, Luke guessed any answers he wanted to get from Sirrus Warman would have to wait until he joined him on the other side.

Luke also knew he had no choice but to go to find out what had eventually come of Joaquin Mateo. It was his last chance. After that, well, he'd have to put it down to experience, and leave robbing stagecoaches to other people.

CHAPTER ELEVEN

Donty Moultrin, a gangly, dark-haired youth, had been taught never to retaliate against a woman, especially if that woman was your ma. He fought hard to keep his temper, but the surprise of the sting of the blow across his face made it difficult to adhere to those principles. He pushed his hands deep in the pockets of his breeches.

Mary Moultrin's face coloured red with rage and her brown eyes flared in anger as she clenched and unclenched her fists. She looked as if she'd like to give him another slap.

'Just because you're seventeen, it don't make it right for you to go against my wishes,' she shouted.

Mary Moultrin stepped forward, almost like she wanted her son to fight back, but Donty remained calm and refused to shout at her. He knew they'd had a letter delivered and from her reaction when she opened it, he believed he had a right to know what it was all about.

'What about Uncle Sirrus and his wishes?' he asked.

She ignored the comment. Instead she concentrated on what troubled her instead.

'You had no right to touch my things,' she said.

Donty lowered his blue-grey eyes towards the ground. He knew she was right and she had reason enough to be angry when she'd found him going through some private papers, but that was all. He wouldn't allow her to accuse him of any other wrongdoing.

'Maybe,' he admitted. 'But you have no right to keep the chance of a better life from me.'

'We're all right here,' she countered. 'You think that gold is going to do you any good?'

'I'm going to find out,' Donty said.

'You're a fool. Just like your Uncle Sirrus,' Mary retorted.

Donty defended his uncle. He didn't like all the insults his ma threw in the man's direction.

'He's not so big a fool as you make out. Hasn't he got a load of gold just waiting for us to find it?'

'You think that gold is any good? How do you know that it even exists? Why didn't he send it to you? Why dig a hole in the ground and hide it?'

Donty couldn't answer any of the questions his ma, the letter and the map raised, but he aimed to find out.

'I'm going to find the gold,' he stated.

'Please don't be foolish,' Mary implored. She tried to reason with him when her threats hadn't worked. 'You have a place to inherit here. At least this is honest. Something you can see and feel . . . unlike that dream Sirrus sent us.'

Donty looked round at the place that barely sustained them throughout the year. He shook his head.

'Ma,' he pleaded, 'come West with me. We can find a much better life than this.'

As he spoke he knew it was useless. Mary Moultrin's two cousins Emmett and Sirrus, had left the homestead many years before. Donty hadn't seen his Uncle Sirrus or Uncle Emmett since he was a young 'un but he'd heard his ma talk about them. She weaved a kind of mystery about them as she interspersed her bitterness at her loss of two relations to gold fever and wove in threads of childhood adventures when she spoke about them. Today, she could find no good words to describe them. When she opened her mouth Donty knew what his ma would say. He'd heard it all before.

'They had gold fever. Lost any shred of good sense they had,' she spat the words out.

'Uncle Sirrus is making it up to us now,' Donty said.

It was as if he hadn't spoken because she went on, 'And now it seems the fever has infected you.'

Donty saw his ma had hardened her heart towards him. Her eyes narrowed and sparkled with bitterness but it didn't matter what she said to Donty. The seeds of adventure had found fertile ground and started to grow.

Donty Moultrin knew he had to find a way from Illinois, where his family had settled many generations ago, to Marysville, on the other side of the country. Every spare moment he toyed with the idea of how he'd travel to Westport in Missouri to find a wagon train, but he knew the cost was out of his league. Unless he could find a lone woman who needed some help with the journey overland, and who would take on a young stranger? He even dreamed about the journey in his sleep. But all his dreams seemed futile.

Although Donty kicked his heels around the homestead for a few more days after the argument with his mother, he knew he'd have to leave. If he wanted to travel overland then it had to be now. It would take several months to reach his destination

81

and he had heard tales of travellers who'd been caught in the cruel winter across the mountains. If he went now then he'd arrive in the fall. There had also been too many harsh words said between him and his ma. At the moment an uneasy truce existed, so fragile it could easily break and shatter into a thousand arguments.

Then something caught his attention when he went into town on an errand. It seemed like the answer to a prayer. The next morning Donty got up, well before the sun appeared near the horizon. He stopped outside the bedroom door and heard the soft steady sound of his ma, sound asleep. For a moment he hesitated, he wanted just to try one more time to get her to see sense. He raised his hand to knock on the door, but then something deep inside him made him realize he'd never change her mind and he turned away. Donty took some bread and beef jerky, and saddled his horse in the stables. He hated going without saying goodbye, but at least, he consoled himself, his ma would have one less mouth to feed.

The advertisement in the local newspaper, for riders to deliver mail, paying fifty dollars a month, all found, to travel for Ben Halladay's Overland Mail and Express Company to San Francisco, had been especially written for him, he decided.

Gilbert Burns, the hirer, wasn't of the same mind, however. He stroked his close-trimmed beard and contemplated the eager young man who stood in front of him.

'You look like something between hay and grass,' he laughed.

'Don't you laugh at me.' Donty's voice rose imperceptibly. 'I'm full grown.'

'How old are you?'

'I'm seventeen, nearly eighteen.'

Only half a head separated them in height. Donty was skinny but strong from all the physical work he'd done on the homestead.

'Tell you what,' Gilbert Burns laughed, 'come back in say, eighteen months' time and I'm sure you'll have no problems getting me to take you on.'

Donty bristled at the insult. 'I can do the job.' He refused to take no for an answer. 'I know how to handle a horse.'

'I'm sure you'll try. But, sorry, it's hard out there and even strong men have been known to break down under the trials they face.'

Donty's jaw set stubbornly. 'I'll stay here until you take me on.'

Another company, the Pony Express, had only taken young men, but the mail route was hard and Ben Halladay's company preferred more mature men. It had started back in 1858 and now had been mainly superseded by Wells and Fargo coaches and telegraph, but there was still a call for the fast personal letter. And as long as folks could pay for it, they'd provide the service. The man turned away. He'd see how long it took before the kid got fed up.

It was two days later that Gilbert Burns noticed Donty Moultrin still waiting on the porch outside his office. Donty sat, back against the wood building, and watched as men trooped back and forth to apply to become a member of the team of ten men wanted for the job.

Burns looked at the determined young man and sighed.

'You're persistent. I'll give you that son,' he said. 'OK. I'll take the risk. I need another body to make up the team.'

Donty jumped to his feet immediately.

'I won't let you down.'

'Best not,' Gilbert Burns threatened. 'Else I'll be chasing you and I'll skin your hide.'

Although it took a comparatively short time, and put fifty dollars a month in his pocket, it took a lot of strength and endurance to cross overland from Illinois to Yuba County.

After Donty had badgered Burns to take him on,

he explained that he aimed to go straight across country.

'And return the same way,' he added.

But of course both knew it was a one-way ticket. Still, Gilbert Burns was only interested in getting the mail delivered, and there were always men who'd travel overland. And if Donty Moultrin wanted to use it for his own ends then it was fine by him as long as he did the job he was paid for.

'I'll pay your money into the bank at San Francisco,' Gilbert Burns told Donty, 'that way I know you won't run off with the first fifty dollars I pay you.'

'What happens if there's no money in the bank when I get there?' the young man asked.

'Why, sunny boy,' Burns chuckled, 'you got a mighty long ride back.'

Donty joined in the laughter. He trusted the big feller. The man had made a business of getting mail delivered so why would he jeopardize it?

However, Burns turned serious again as he asked Donty, 'What happens if this uncle of yours don't give you a welcome?'

CHAPTER TWELVE

The thought had crossed Donty's mind about the welcome he might receive from his kin's family. If his ma could hold such hatred in her heart then did it mean his Uncle Emmett could be an awkward cuss as well? Donty Moultrin shrugged his shoulders. He'd have to cross that bridge later. He had to find the place first because he wasn't sure exactly where it was. Uncle Sirrus's letter was post marked Marysville but there was nothing more to indicate exactly where Warman's Longhorn Ranch was located.

He hadn't told Burns too much, as helpful as the feller had been when he hired him, he felt it showed no sense to let people know you were after a pot of gold. No sense at all.

He'd fared well with the weather throughout the journey, or he would say, he'd got used to the sun, wind, rain and snow that battered his skin to leather and made it weatherproof.

When the last stage of his journey was almost over, Donty Moultrin began to smell like a pig waiting for slaughter, with a hot stinking aroma drifting up from his hide.

'Best find myself a hot barrel of suds,' he confided to the horse who'd been his companion for the last forty-eight hours.

At every leg of the journey, a fresh mount was provided, and this horse was coming to the end of the road, as was indeed Donty, who felt his bones rattle with each step they took. He'd had a few days' rest at each station before he'd taken the packages onwards. There were stations dotted all over the trail through to San Francisco although Donty wouldn't complete the chain. He hoped he'd be able to draw some money at the Marysville bank to tide him over for a while. He'd had a longer ride than he'd ever had before and thought that when he peeled off his leather chaps and wool breeches, he'd find calluses the size of dinner plates on his thighs.

Donty had invested in a pair of thick leather gloves before he'd set off, a good buy, or his hands would've been no more than shredded skin. He protected his head as much as possible with a wide-brimmed felt hat, but his face had still caught the sun and turned it the colour of peanut butter. A scrawny kid to start with, however the journey had matured him into a strong handsome man with a tight and muscular body and arms that bulged out when he gripped the reins.

As he finally entered the town of Marysville, even though he felt he looked like a dime's worth of dog's meat, quite a few young ladies turned and looked at him in admiration. He didn't notice. He was so tired and full of trail dust that when he stabled his horse and handed on his post to the next man and his duty discharged, all he wanted to do was to clean up and change clothes. He drew some cash without any problems, bought a pair of buckskin pants for $2.25 and a cotton shirt for £1.50 before he headed for the bath house. Only then, he decided, could he go and locate his Uncle Emmett.

'You're in luck.'

The bath house, a small fenced-off area, set behind the saloon bar, beckoned to him. Brimful of barrels, it offered a taste of luxury to Donty Moultrin. A notice nailed onto the makeshift door boasted that no more than three people used the water before it got changed.

The man who made the comment looked up as Donty entered the bath house. He topped up the barrel with boiling water.

'This has only been used once. And he needed it about as much as a preacher on Sunday,' he said.

Donty paid fifty cents, shucked off his clothes and soaked in the water until he felt cleaner than a fish in a bowl.

After that everything caught his attention in Marysville. Big, busy and booming, it was a hive of activity. The town had grown out of the gold rush era. Some men, Donty knew from the letters his ma had received from her brother, had invested it right back. His Uncle Emmett had bought some land and built a ranch in Yuba County and provided employment for those who wanted it. He gave work to the local Indians, although Mary Moultrin made that sound like he'd made a pact with the devil.

'Don't know why he's got to associate with Redskins,' she'd commented.

But it was a simple fact that most of the whites preferred panning and digging for gold and he needed someone to do the work.

Those letters had got fewer and fewer over the years. Donty suspected that after a while, the effort of sending stuff into a void grew too much. He'd tried to write a letter to Uncle Emmett once, but after he'd had his breeches warmed with a hickory switch, he never attempted it again. That reminded Donty Moultrin to post another letter to his ma. They'd parted on bad terms but he hadn't forgotten she'd bought him up alone, and still deserved his respect. He had handed in a letter at the main store to be delivered when he left town, and promised her he'd always let her know how things were. Then he walked round the building until he got to the entrance of the saloon. He had a good thirst and he could do with a hunk of bread and some hog meat to fill his belly.

'They don't serve milk drinks here, boy.'

The man who'd made the jibe, Joaquin Mateo, well known for trouble, spat towards the spittoon, and missed.

Donty Moultrin's face flushed dark red at the insult. He'd asked for a drink and got laughed at. His fingers gripped at the wooden bar.

'I ain't asked for that,' he said. 'I just want a drink of beer and some food.'

The barman gave the young man a glass of beer. He didn't want any trouble. However, the one who'd made the remark about milk felt ready for a game. He came almost nose to nose with Donty.

'You smell prettier than a girl,' he said.

The huge intake of breath which greeted that insult made one or two wonder if there was enough air left to breathe. Others at the bar shuffled further away, not sure how the young stranger would react to all this, and they didn't want to get caught in a mêlée.

Donty Moultrin's tormentor put down his glass of whiskey, and his one good hand moved towards his gun belt. He had one good hand and a reputation for using it with some speed on the draw. Before Donty Moultrin had a chance to react he heard another man speak out in his defence. Joaquin Mateo knew the dapper, well-dressed man immediately and his presence made him wary.

'The boy isn't armed,' Soames Ho warned. 'So I suggest you finish your drink and leave him alone.'

There weren't many men who felt comfortable about challenging Joaquin Mateo. All who had had paid a heavy price and regretted it, because they were now six feet under in Boot Hill cemetery. Yet as Joaquin stared back into the two slightly upturned eyes of the man who'd spoken, he thought twice about facing him out. It wasn't only the hard look of the man who stood by the youngster, it was the strange feeling that the two had met somewhere before. Joaquin couldn't remember where they'd met and he didn't like being at a disadvantage. There were gaps in his memory since he'd been found half-dead in the Sierra foothills and nursed back to health by the Indians. However when he looked at his useless arm, he sometimes wished they'd left him there to die. The injury had twisted his already cruel mind and now he was crazier than a run-over raccoon. But he sandwiched his anger and tried to spit it out as a joke. His snarl turned into a twisted grin.

'I'm only giving the boy a bit of a roasting,' Joaquin Mateo said.

The oriental man didn't push his advantage. He wasn't about to look for a fight with Joaquin Mateo, at least not yet.

Soames Ho matched the other man's smile.

'That's OK, friend. But we'll all get on with finishing our drinks now.'

There were no gaps in Soames Ho's memory. He knew exactly where he'd seen Joaquin Mateo. But he wanted him and the gold and one wrong move might end the quest he'd set himself.

Joaquin nodded and threw back his whiskey before he wiped his mouth with the back of his hand. As Donty Moultrin and Soames Ho watched the man leave, they both knew they'd made an enemy.

'I didn't need any help,' the boy said.

He had yet to learn that sometimes you did, and a simple thanks was appreciated. Soames Ho turned away and went back to his drink. He was in no hurry to speak to the young whippersnapper. Then it seemed that Donty remembered the good things his ma had taught him.

'Thanks anyway, mister,' he said.

The thanks, although given grudgingly, was acknowledged. The man who'd stopped a nasty incident between Donty and Joaquin turned back to the boy and stuck out his hand in friendship.

'Soames Ho,' he introduced himself.

He saw a young man, tall, lean, muscular and the spitting image of Sirrus Warman. Soames Ho hoped he didn't prove to be as feckless and crooked as his uncle.

'I'm Donty Moultrin. I'm on my way to visit my uncle, Emmett Warman.'

Soames Ho knew this. He kept his eyes wide open and his ears to the ground for any information about the Warman clan. And usually it came quickly to his notice. He didn't live anywhere permanent in Marysville now. He'd never been back to the homestead since he'd left it because to him it was full of too many bad memories. And because, as a Pinkerton agent, he constantly moved around the area of California, he never called anywhere home. That way he got to know a lot of people and a lot of information. Tonight he bunked at Lil's House and she had a reputation for serving the best baked chicken, rice and sweet corn in the West. He invited the boy to sup with him. His reasons weren't all social; he wanted to find out exactly what the boy knew about the gold. And Soames Ho reasoned he must know something – surely he wouldn't travel all this way just for a visit.

Although Donty Moultrin wanted to find the ranch as soon as possible he accepted the man's invitation to supper. He decided there was plenty of time tomorrow. Now his stomach rumbled and reminded him he was hungry and felt as thin as someone, who, if they closed one eye, would be mistaken for a needle.

'I'd like that, Mr Ho. I surely would.'

He hadn't guessed the reason for the man's generosity. He knew nothing about the fact that the gold had eluded Soames Ho for almost a year and hadn't left his mind.

Soames Ho was as determined as ever to find out where it was stashed. It was still around, of that he had no doubt. It was evident from Joaquin Mateo, who never usually lasted longer in one place than a pint of whiskey in a poker game, that the gold was hereabouts. From what Soames Ho had gleaned about him, Joaquin normally hit the first bank and high tailed it out of town.

And, of course, Soames Ho knew that in the shadows the vaporous figure of Luke Yale, also known as Lode Pinkerton, waited. He'd followed Joaquin Mateo on a couple of occasions and had seen the pair together. Luke Yale, associated with the gold, kept a low profile. It suited Soames Ho to sit it out. If he hauled him in, then he'd never find the gold. So all he did was watch and wait.

He knew enough to not be too nosy. At least, that is, not openly because men came out West to find a new life. If he asked too many direct questions he might end up spitting out lead. He could wait because he knew the time would come for action.

Soames Ho would be ready.

CHAPTER THIRTEEN

As soon as Donty Moultrin found out whereabouts his Uncle Emmett's ranch was situated, a few miles out of town, he set out. The ranch, big, bold and the only building in miles of grassland, soon loomed up in front of him.

The place, a two-storey log and schist rock construction with a shingle roof, had cream calico blinds at the window. Those must've been fashioned by the hand of his cousin Grace because Donty couldn't image any man who'd sit down and sew curtains. Much more practical, he thought, an outbuilding used as a chicken run and placed right next to the kitchen. They wouldn't have far to go from pen to pot, he observed.

He had Uncle Sirrus's letter in his waistcoat pocket and it almost burnt a hole right through the fabric.

Donty couldn't wait to start hunting for treasure but when he got near to the main house he got a reception he hadn't expected.

'Get off my land.' A man stood with a shotgun pointed straight at him. 'I've had enough of strangers calling here lately. So turn around and get going.'

The young man sat on his horse, open-mouthed. He took in the brown eyes and the mouth which curled down at the edges. Just like his mother.

'Uncle Emmett, I'm Donty Moultrin, your cousin Mary's son.'

'Don't care who you say you are. I want you off my land.'

'You're just like my ma. She has that same darn stubborn way about her.'

In less time than it took to swipe a gnat off a sore spot, Donty found he'd been hauled off the horse and thrown onto the ground. The older man didn't take no cussing from anyone. The boy wiped a hand across his mouth and found blood on it from his split lip.

'Don't you speak to me like that, whoever you say you are,' Emmett Warman said.

Donty decided an apology could be the best way to deal with the situation. No good being thrown off the ranch before he had a chance to make friends with kin.

'Sorry, sir.'

'Get up.'

Emmett Warman waved the shotgun around so Donty took heed of his instructions and scrambled to his feet. He brushed the dirt from his new buckskin pants. Then he started to explain the reason for his visit.

'I got a letter from Uncle Sirrus,' he said. 'He said he wanted to see me.'

He stood up and dusted himself down then took the paper from his waistcoat pocket and handed it over. Emmett shook it open and glanced at it before throwing it back to Donty.

'I think you've come to look for gold.'

Donty smiled and nodded in reply.

'Seemed good reason enough for visiting,' he added. 'And I wanted to see you again, Uncle Emmett.'

'Well, you're not welcome here. Your Uncle Sirrus brought nothing but trouble with that dream of his. You're just in a long line of people who've been here to sniff out some buried treasure.' Emmett turned his back on the young man. 'And even if you are my cousin's son I don't want you here.'

'I want at least to see Uncle Sirrus before I go.'

Emmet Warman stared, then hesitated as it was obvious from the boy's comments he wouldn't know what had happened to his uncle.

'Oh sorry, son, your Uncle Sirrus got shot full of lead and went to meet his Maker. You'll find him up that hill. His only claim to fame, boy, is that he's the first Warman buried here.'

Donty looked mortified at the revelation, and yet he supposed he ought to have expected it. No one gives someone else his gold if he's able to enjoy it.

'Pa.'

Donty, shaken by his uncle's words, looked up towards the side of the house as a girl's voice called out.

'You can't turn him away. He's the image of Uncle Sirrus,' she continued. 'And we're his kin. We don't turn away kin. And you can see he's upset by the news.'

Donty smiled faintly at his friendly advocate. This must be his second cousin Grace. She looked more attractive than he'd expected her to be. She was either oblivious of her pa's scowl or she plain just ignored it anyway.

Grace strode up to Donty and placed her hand on his arm. In the year since Sirrus Warman had died, his niece, Grace, had blossomed into an attractive feisty young woman who dared to challenge her pa's authority with impunity.

'Yes. And he's got your Uncle Sirrus's personality.

He's come to California to get rich, but not through hard work,' Emmett bit back at his outrageous daughter.

Donty Moultrin spluttered with indignation at the insult.

'That's not fair. I sure know how to work. I rode with Ben Halladay's Pony Express all the way from Illinois.'

'Take my advice kid,' his Uncle Emmett said, 'you go ride all the way back again.'

'Go on with you, Pa,' Grace said.

She refused to believe that her pa would turn his sights away from his own kin. She wanted to know all about Donty and her Aunt Mary, a shadowy figure she'd heard about but never met. She edged Donty towards Emmett and pushed her hand through her pa's folded arms and smiled up at him. The two men were hauled closer to each other than they wanted to be.

'Let's at least invite your cousin Mary's son into our home for a drink and a bite of supper tonight.'

While his Uncle Emmett didn't exactly welcome Donty, he knew he couldn't turn the boy away because he'd never do that even to a stranger. By the time they'd all eaten a meal cooked by Grace and had washed it down with beer, he was relaxed enough to be civil.

'I take it your ma ain't planning to join you out here?' Emmett asked. Donty shook his head.

'No, sir. She wanted to stay on the homestead. She said she belonged there.'

'She was never one who liked change,' Emmett commented. 'I wanted her to come West with us, especially after her hubby died. But as you say, she's set in her ways. I'm surprised she let you come here.'

He wiped the gravy from his mouth with a cloth and waited for the boy to answer.

Donty looked down at the floor.

'I see.'

Donty wondered if Uncle Emmett would definitely order him home now, but the older man sighed and got up from the table. 'I'm off to do some chores,' he said. 'And if you intend to stay, I expect you to work as well. You've come at the right time. We need to round up the cattle before winter sets in. You'll start first thing in the morning.'

'I will, sir.' Donty replied.

He felt relieved that his Uncle Emmett didn't say he ought to send him home. He'd have time to look for buried treasure now. Grace's voice cut through his thoughts as soon as her pa had left the room. She sidled up to him and suggested they sit on the porch so they could talk privately. She'd changed from her split skirt and rough hewn top and now wore a

101

muslin dress and smelled of lavender. Donty
squirmed uncomfortably in his chair. He wondered if
she was aware of the effect she had on him but as he
looked at the innocent smile she gave him as they
perused the map she'd sent him all those months
ago, he dismissed the idea.

'After I posted the letter to you I wished I'd copied
the map. I would've been away by now.'

'Oh yes,' he commented, 'perhaps it's just as well
you hadn't got the map, because I'd have been
chasing after you and we'd have met on different
terms.'

'What do you mean?' Grace queried.

'Uncle Sirrus left the gold to me,' Donty said.

'They say "finders' keepers".' Grace's smile
disappeared, then in an instant it was back and she
reached out towards him. 'Hey, let's not quarrel. We
can both go look for the gold tomorrow.'

'I'll have to wait for a day off if I'm working for
Uncle Emmett.'

'No, Pa said he'll send you off to round up strays.
We can find plenty of cattle by the Sierra foothills.'
Grace smiled mischievously. 'I believe that's where
Uncle Sirrus said the gold should be.'

Next day Donty waited for Grace to join him. He'd
rather have gone off on his own, but, although he
had the map, Grace knew the area better than he

102

did, and that would shorten the search. The air was fresh and cool and his breath came out in puffs like clouds. He pushed away the fanciful thought and buttoned up his shirt and drew the collar of his jacket up to keep the draught away from his neck. The sun had just started to warm the air, when Grace showed up. She pulled her horse next to his.

'Won't your pa miss you?' Donty asked.

'Told him I had to go to town for provisions. Everyone's got bread and cold meat at noon and there's a stew cooking in the stove for supper.'

Grace, resourceful if nothing else, constantly surprised Donty. Before he could ask her any other questions, she clicked her tongue and spurred her horse forward up the treacherous track. Although the horses were sure-footed as they made their way up the Sierra paths, Grace didn't blanch once as they looked down into the valley whenever they stopped and consulted the map. Eventually, it was Donty who said they'd be better off if they tethered their mounts in a clearing, and walked the rest of the way.

'According to this we ought to be able to find where the gold is hidden.' He looked across the tree line. 'Yes, over there.'

They followed the trail excitedly only to be disappointed yet again. The same thing had happened throughout the day.

103

'Uncle Sirrus drew the map from memory when he was ill,' Grace warned, 'so I'm not sure how accurate it is.'

Very inaccurate, Donty Moultrin thought, as they paced round in circles. It was a day wasted as far as he was concerned.

Later, on his journey home, as luck would have it, he found four steers and brought them back to the ranch. At least Uncle Emmet wouldn't suspect that he'd been out on the trail of the gold. Grace had left him as soon as they decided to call it a day, and arrived home earlier. He heard her bang the gong for supper. His stomach was empty and glad of the rich buffalo stew Grace said she'd thrown together. He liked the taste her of cooking however she said she'd concocted it, he thought.

She'd changed out of her riding clothes and put on a plain dress to serve up supper. Donty noticed the nipped-in waist and young blossoming figure. He noticed Uncle Emmett's gaze move across from Grace and then to him.

'Grace makes a good stew,' Donty said.

He knew it sounded lame as soon as he'd said it, but Emmett merely grunted and made no comment.

Donty helped Grace to clear, wash and dry the pots and plates then they sat outside on the porch again and scoured over the map. Donty actually turned it round and round as he tried to make sense of it.

'Do you reckon we been looking in the wrong direction,' he joked.

Grace frowned. She studied the map again.

'You know, you might be right,' she said.

'What?'

'The compass signs are wrong. Uncle Sirrus added them after he'd shown me the map. This is north.'

'I thought you knew the area?'

Her soft pink cheeks flamed red as Donty sneered at her embarrassment.

'Well, anyone can make a little mistake. We can look again tomorrow.'

'I'll go on my own.'

'No, you won't. I've got as much right to that gold as you.'

She didn't give him a chance to reply before she stormed away angrily.

In the heated exchange, neither Donty nor Grace noticed that someone else had listened in on their plans.

CHAPTER FOURTEEN

Light Weaver's brother, Moon Bear, scooped the ground with his hand and let the soil slip through his fingers. He sniffed at the residue under his nails and knew no one had been there since the moon had been full in the sky many times. He could see the earth had been disturbed, and his heart was heavy because its disturbance coincided with the time Light Weaver had gone out and not returned.

The tribe had suspected that her disappearance had something to do with the white men who lived around them. They'd taken everything from them: their land, their sacred places of worship and the burial places of their ancestors. Sometimes they took their women. The Indians no longer worked on the neighbouring ranches. The elders had decreed it because they believed no one would be safe until Light Weaver's spirit returned to her home.

The boundary of the cave stank of the animals that had inhabited it or had been brought here to be devoured by their predators. The smell of bear pierced through his nostrils over all others, but Moon Bear had no fear of the creature. Many seasons ago he had killed a hungry bear which had prowled around their village at night-time. Although a young boy, his arrows had found its mark as the bear silhouetted against the moon, set him an easy target. The creature had been toppled with a well-aimed shot. He'd been given the name out of honour for his deeds and acknowledgement of his passage into manhood.

He could also detect his sister. Somewhere underneath the soil and rocks, Light Weaver lay. He closed his eyes and invoked the wrath of the gods he worshipped to give him strength enough to face the task before him.

As he worked Moon Bear became aware of another distinctive smell, a man's smell, and the hair on the back of his scalp rose as he recognized it. He'd swear on his life or those of his tribe that he knew this scent. He remembered when they'd found a man on their way back from a hunt. Almost dead from his wounds, in the foothills of the Sierra they had carried him back and the tribe had nursed him to health. This was the man who'd been here in this cave.

However, before they were able to ask him any questions, he'd disappeared with the help of a companion. The man had waited until the braves were away from camp on a hunt and the women busy with their work, and then he'd swooped in and helped his friend escape. They hadn't considered it necessary to mount guard on the man they'd found near to death in the mountains. The wound he had was from the gun of a white man.

Now Moon Bear cursed himself for his part in the man's recovery. He discovered too late that the man was evil. His heart felt heavy inside his chest as he moved the rocks then dug his hands in the ground and looked for his missing sister.

An hour later, Light Weaver lay in his arms. Carefully he wrapped her body in a blanket and laid it across his horse's back. He'd also found the gold the white men coveted, but he left that in the ground. Moon Bear promised his sister he'd be back; he'd find her murderer and exact a vengeance for the loss of her life.

CHAPTER FIFTEEN

Both Donty and Grace were blissfully unaware that they were not the only ones who were interested in their quest for buried treasure and that the gold was important to more than just the two of them. Young and inexperienced, they didn't notice others who watched their actions and listened to their conversations.

The previous evening it had been Al Brown, Emmett Warman's foreman, who had sat and listened to the two young 'uns. He'd been unnoticed, hat pulled down, as he sat and snoozed outside on the porch after supper. He had a fairly privileged position in the household, not only as the foreman, but as a good friend of Emmett. He'd been with him since he started his cattle business a few miles out of Marysville and they supped and jawed together most evenings. And that night after Emmett had gone to bed he heard Donty and Grace discuss the map Sirrus Warman had sent to Donty.

A feller called Greed, a green-eyed monster, had nestled up to Al Brown and now sat companionably beside him.

And for many others it proved the same; when Sirrus Warman's nephew came into town it was like a dream come true.

Joaquin Mateo chewed at his wad of tobacco and frequently spat a pool of yellow liquid onto the ground. Sometimes he missed his aim and the spittle dribbled down the front of his shirt and pants and splattered his boots. No one dared to point it out.

He, too, had kept an eye on Donty Moultrin and waited for him to make a move.

Today he waited in the Sierra foothills again. He leant against a tree and wished the time would move quicker than he knew it could. He watched his horse graze and waited for the two fool kids to show up again. He knew for certain they had knowledge of the gold. Why else would they be so intent on the map? He'd reasoned that if Sirrus Warman had revealed the whereabouts of the gold to anybody, his bet was on the girl and boy.

Yesterday he watched them going round in circles and had half a mind to jump out and confront them.

110

In fact when they stopped to consult the map he almost stepped out to do just that, but a sixth sense made him reconsider. He didn't want to go and kill them yet, not through any sense of compassion, but because he didn't want to be chased by a posse, led by a furious uncle. He had a theory that a furious Emmett Warman would beat him up so hard there wouldn't be enough left of him to snore if he harmed his daughter and nephew. It had never happened to him but he'd heard kin could raise hell if anything happened to their own.

Joaquin Mateo only wanted to fill his saddle-bags with the loot from the robbery and get clean away from these parts with everything he'd got intact.

Now he shook his head and wondered if he'd made the wrong decision. Perhaps it had been a mistake not to shoot the two of them, because now he'd have a map and be able to find the gold a whole lot quicker than two giggly greenhorns.

He kicked his booted foot against the tree in frustration but common sense prevailed again. He had waited so long that he reckoned a few more hours wouldn't matter. He'd only have to wait until the gold surfaced then he'd shoot them both. The waiting game would pay off because he had a plan in mind for that con man, Luke Yale, to take the rap for their murders. A growl in the guise of a laugh escaped his lips. Fool man believed they were buddies. Joaquin only wanted to make sure Luke Yale didn't double-cross him. He'd heard the phrase many years ago and it had stuck in his mind, 'Keep your friends close and your enemies even closer.' Not that he made friends at all but he agreed with the bit about enemies. It made sense to him. He visualized Luke Yale, who would be found with a smoking gun, or at least the gun that had fired the bullets that killed the kids, after he, Joaquin, raised the alarm at the ranch. That way he'd be able to kill several birds with one stone.

Luke Yale also waited for something to happen. At the moment he kept well back away from the action. He only wanted a small piece of gold and didn't think Joaquin Mateo would begrudge him a morsel. After all, it was his information that had got them this far. At first he'd wanted the lion's share of the robbery, but when he weighed up the risks of a fight with Mateo, he knew the outcome wouldn't be too good for him, and dropped the idea. He wasn't as fat as he used to be – all the worry had made him lose his appetite – but he still couldn't match the strength of the man with one arm. He groaned inwardly at the thought that he hadn't got what it took to defend himself against the invalid man. Luke Yale wanted to go far away from this place. He'd have thrown the

112

towel in and left it all to Joaquin at times but he seemed to want him nearby. It was almost as if the feller didn't trust him. Luke Yale shrugged, unable to comprehend Joaquin Mateo's suspicious attitude towards him. Hadn't he proved himself a friend when he got him away from those Redskins?

Only Soames Ho had no bad intentions towards the boy. Yet he knew something bad could happen. He'd waited for a year to get his hands on the gold. It had caused him some indignation to let those outlaws get away with a load of gold whilst he'd only been able to sit helplessly and watch. If those gals hadn't been present on the stagecoach then no way would he have been in this situation now. He'd have waited ten years to get his revenge.

So Soames Ho realized that if he wanted to get his hands on the gold, then there were others who wanted to do the same. Two robbers had died but there were two others still alive and they'd be ready to pounce at the first opportunity. It worried him that the boy could end up hurt. He knew that when Donty Moultrin went off to visit his uncle, he, Soames Ho, had best be close behind him.

CHAPTER SIXTEEN

Grace galloped off on her horse to join Donty on the mountain road. She slipped away as soon as she could from the morning's chores. Emmett Warman watched his daughter hightail it out of the ranch, a blur of red hair, as she sped off on her horse. Had Grace seen the expression on his face she'd have been more wary of her behaviour. As it was, she didn't see Emmett Warman shake his head, and say a silent prayer that his daughter wouldn't get into too much trouble.

In a background of snow-capped mountains, Donty waited for the young woman to appear. His horse scrapped its front hoof against the ground, and mimicked his master's impatience. Donty sat up in his saddle as the horse's ears pricked up. The beast had heard the sound of Grace and her steed gallop along the pass towards them.

'I thought you'd never get here,' Donty grumbled.

The tips of his ears and nose were purple with cold. The buckskin pants tucked into his boots were warm enough but the fresh wind picked at any parts of his body not covered up and turned them into ice. He'd buttoned his shirt and gathered his coat collar closer to him to block out the nip of the north wind. Grace's face, in contrast to Donty's cold skin, flushed up pink with warmth from the exertion of the ride out.

'Told you I'd be here,' she retorted.

Donty steered his horse in the direction they'd decided to search out first.

'Yes,' he said, 'but I thought you'd be here this morning not almost into next week.'

'You grumpy old man,' Grace moaned.

She'd broke a limb hightailing it out here and all she'd earned was a scold face. She fixed her lips into a steely grimace to choke back any more retorts that'd only start an argument, and followed her cousin deeper into the Sierra. Today there would great changes in her life, she thought, and she determined to be right there when it happened. She kept close to Donty.

As they wound their way upwards, and followed the path they'd agreed last night, Donty's features relaxed as his irritation eased. He glanced back and smiled at the spirited girl. He believed she had a deal of spunk to evade her pa and come with him on what might prove to be another wild goose chase. He felt guilty because he'd nigh on bit her head off but she'd had the sense not to prolong the spat and he liked that. Donty recalled all the arguments he'd had at home and the memory of his mother floated into his mind.

He quickly dismissed the image and focused on the map. Then, as he looked upwards, all his concentration moved towards the cave above and to the left of them. In fact for a moment Donty didn't know whether it was a cave or just the shadow of a jutting rock face. He looked towards the sun and had a notion it was far to low in the sky to cause a shadow like that. He put his hand up to stop Grace in her tracks.

'We might be here,' Donty said.

He kept his voice low. As far as he was concerned, no one else was about to hear him, but he acted like that all the same, aware of the enormity of the find. If indeed they had discovered the whereabouts of the gold.

'It depends whether we placed the compass on the right place on the map.'

He finished the sentence with a soft, nervous

chuckle. Grace flexed her knees and steered her horse to sit along side him.

'You've found it? What are we waiting for?' she asked. 'I want to feel the gold in my hands.'

'Uncle Sirrus left the gold to me,' Donty said.

Grace pulled on her horse's reins.

'He's my uncle too. And I nursed him when he got sick.' She pushed past him and then slipped from the saddle. She slapped her horse's rump gently to get him to move to some grazing pasture. 'I'm going up there.'

Donty Moultrin jumped off his horse. 'You wait for me,' he admonished, 'there's no telling what's round here.'

But Grace ignored him and started to move towards the hollow. Donty sighed. She was headstrong, he thought. He at least had enough sense to get a couple of shovels, and an oil lamp, off his horse's saddle. His hand hovered over the shotgun. He took that as well.

'One of us best be prepared,' he muttered.

Five minutes later they both stood at the edge of the cave. Grace Warman peered dubiously inside the entrance. She wrinkled her nose.

'Sure smells bad inside there,' she said.

Donty agreed. And if this was the right place, he didn't want to stay one moment longer than necessary. Donty scraped the flint against the sole of his boot. The sudden flash of light illuminated the worried features of his companion. His attitude softened towards her. Although she acted high and mighty she was still a frightened young girl.

'You'll be all right with me,' he said.

Donty smiled at her as he lit the lamp. She didn't return the smile, annoyed he'd caught her off guard.

'I can look after myself,' she said. 'I don't need a boy to hold my hand.'

Exasperated, he laughed out loud at her quip. And she joined him with a giggle. He held out one of the shovels he'd brought with him. His voice gruff, he ordered her to get to work.

'Get digging then, little girl.'

They could both see where the ground had been disturbed. There were small rocks strewn everywhere, and a fresh mound of dirt flattened into the ground by what looked like bare feet. It was as if someone had been here before them but hadn't completed the job. However, Donty could see that they'd still have plenty of work to do and thrust his shovel into the ground.

'You start at that end,' he instructed Grace, 'no sense in clashing iron together. You give off enough sparks without making more.'

He knew she'd want to add some to his comment

but he didn't want to be distracted, so he immediately put his head down and started on with the task. Grace stood and watched him for a moment, and then she shrugged and started work. Time enough for arguments later, and more, she decided.

Soon both had sweat trickling down their faces. The place was airless and stuffy and the work added to the heat inside the cave. Grace's face got streaked with dirt as she tried to keep her hair away from her eyes. Donty said she looked like a skunk and ducked when she threw a shovel full of dirt at him but it didn't stop his taunts.

'Great place for a winter sleep,' he commented.

Grace looked up, wiped her forehead again, and stared at him quizzically.

'What do you mean?'

The slight tremble in her voice told him she knew the answer to the question as it formed on her lips.

'There are plenty of grizzly bears around here. I bet one has made it his own private sleeping quarters.'

The smirk on his face told Grace that he didn't seriously believe a bear would race into the cave to claim its territory; nevertheless, she resumed her work at a faster pace. Grace's shovel hit the box first. The 'clang' vibrated through the cave and made the girl jump nervously. She stopped her task and stared at the edge of the green box as if it was about to jump out and bite her. Donty looked up and wondered what was wrong. The quip about girls not being able to work hard never left his lips as he became aware of what she'd found.

'This is it,' she cried.

Donty rushed towards her, jumped into the ditch she'd made, and feverishly unearthed the box. They didn't notice anything amiss as they both scrabbled into the hole and pulled out the box which had been under the buck board of the stagecoach.

'We did it!' Donty and Grace shouted together.

'How do we open the thing?' Grace asked.

Their joy turned to sobriety as they saw the large lock which held it shut.

'I suppose a saw, or a plain old blast from a shot gun will release its grip.'

'Don't worry about that, you young 'uns.'

Both Donty Moultrin and Grace Warman turned and looked towards the mouth of the cave where the voice came from. Donty recognized him from the saloon bar. Even the wide-brimmed hat didn't disguise that mean scarred face that now threatened them. The man, although he only had one good arm, used it well and he pointed his shotgun at them. Donty thought about the gun he'd left leaning against the wall of the cave. He'd been foolish enough to leave it behind when he'd raced across the cave, full of heady enthusiasm, to the box of gold. He knew, too late, he should have kept the gun within arm's reach.

'Don't even think about doing anything foolish.'

It seemed Mateo sensed that Donty might try something stupid. Joaquin Mateo held his gun out as if to emphasize the control he had over the two of them. His jaw worked on his wad of baccy before he spat out the juice.

'Unless, of course, you want to end up with a belly full of lead.'

Donty shook his head. That was the last thing he wanted. He'd hardly be able to help Grace if he got shot dead. He saw no sense in a one-sided fight with this man.

'No, sir,' he said.

'Then let's get this box out of this place and load it onto the horse outside.'

Donty fancied that Joaquin Mateo had no intention of leaving them to tell tales when he left, but he'd make them help him some first. He knew he'd have to wait for the right opportunity to escape. But for now he'd do as he was told.

'You shouldn't help him,' Grace snarled. Her voice overflowed with indignation because Donty hadn't tried to put up a fight. 'And why call him Sir? You could've dived for that shotgun. . . .'

'I always call someone with a gun pointed at me, Sir. And I suggest you do that, or would you prefer to see us both splattered over the cave walls as a snack for that bear?'

'Hey, you two, cut out the jawing,' Joaquin Mateo called out. 'Get on with moving that box.'

'Yes, sir. It's a bit heavy for the little girl.' He answered the man yet in a lower voice he spoke to Grace. 'We got to find a chance to get away from him . . . and take it. So shut up and do as I say.'

Grace's face sent out the message that she wasn't too pleased with the way he'd spoke to her, but she did 'shut up' and went along with him. After all, she'd nothing better to suggest. Outside they both had to shade their eyes against the glare of the daylight as they placed the box at their feet. When Donty opened his eyes again he saw that they had another addition to the group.

From the expression on Joaquin Mateo's face, they could see he wasn't expecting company. His face told them all he was none too pleased to see the man.

'I thought I told you to wait until I came to pick you up,' he said.

The fat man astride a tired horse merely inclined his head and touched his hat politely. He acted as if he was at a Sunday picnic. But the two youngsters could sense the tension between the two men.

'No sense in doing that, friend,' Luke Yale answered. 'I thought you might like some help. That's a mighty heavy box there. I can take my share straight off. You know, to help you out some.'

'No need to do that. I'll take care of this and come back for you.'

'Oh, it's no trouble, friend. And since I'm here I'll stay and give you a hand.'

Luke's lips turned upwards into a sneer as he looked pointedly at the stump that used to be Joaquin Mateo's hand. He knew Joaquin hadn't noticed him as he passed by. However Luke had been full of curiosity about what his erstwhile companion was up to. And now he'd found out. The kids had discovered the gold and here was Joaquin Mateo, ready to take it off their hands. He looked at the other man's shifty eyes, narrow as slits yet brimful of threats, as they stared up at him. He knew full well that Joaquin Mateo's only intention was to ride as far away as he could and as fast as possible. His hand moved slowly down towards the small derringer in his boot.

CHAPTER SEVENTEEN

Donty Moultrin watched the two men. He guessed one of them was about to make a move. Neither wanted to do the honourable thing and share the booty. Honourable from his point of view because he'd heard there was no honour amongst thieves.

Donty surmised that when the men had a shoot out, he and Grace had to run. It would be their only chance to escape.

He guardedly looked round at the landscape. If they ran towards the horses, they'd be too exposed. It might be better to seek shelter back in the cave. At least his gun was still in there. And after Joaquin Mateo and Luke Yale had settled their dispute, it would probably only leave one to fend off.

Joaquin understood that Luke Yale wasn't about to fall for his friendly talk. His hand went to his belt and tightened over his .44 Peacemaker.

Luke Yale watched the movement of the other man's hand. That gun might blast a hole in his chest, he thought, but not if I can shoot a bullet through his eye first. In an almost imperceptible movement he slid his fingers into the side of his boot towards his trusty little derringer.

'I've waited far too long to get this gold,' Joaquin said. 'I'm not about to give any of it up.'

Donty Moultrin watched Joaquin Mateo and the fat man carefully. He wanted to be ready for any move the two men made.

'I did a fool thing taking you from the Indians,' Luke Yale said. 'Shows it don't do to be humane.'

Joaquin Mateo lifted his gun as the other man spoke. 'You're right there,' he said. 'Too much humanity ain't good for you.'

He fired as he spoke.

The derringer spat out its bullet.

Donty didn't wait for the outcome. They were off as soon as the guns splattered out their ammo.

'Run, Grace.'

Donty pointed towards the cave. For once Grace didn't bother to argue. Instinctively, they both grabbed hold of the box they'd just hauled from the cave.

'That was a dang fool thing to do,' Donty and Grace said almost together as they hid in the shadows.

'They're gonna come after us now,' Donty said.

'It's our gold,' Grace said.

Donty didn't reply. He went back to the place he'd left his shot gun. He knew he'd need it now. Outside they heard the sound of guns fired across the Sierra. Donty Moultrin prayed silently that his Uncle Emmett or one of his men would hear the gun shots and investigate. He knew that he and Grace would not be able to leave this place without a fight. But he'd like to think some kind of help was on its way.

There were several other people who heard the roar of gunfire.

Soames Ho followed the trail the young ones had taken earlier in the day. His ears pricked up at the unexpected noise. He hurried his horse with a click of his tongue to encourage it to quicken the pace. He had no idea what to expect but he prayed that Donty and his cousin Grace were all right.

Moon Bear had returned to seek out the murderer of his sister, after he'd seen her body delivered to the gods. Now he wanted to avenge her death. He heard the shots and knew they came from the direction of the cave.

Outside the cave Joaquin Mateo stood over Luke

126

Yale. He sneered as he kicked the body over and saw the hole where the slugs had left a jagged mess. The derringer lay in the dead man's hand.

'Think you were gonna best me?' he grunted in disgust.

The man was a fool as far as he was concerned and now he was a dead fool. Joaquin kicked the body away so it rolled towards the undergrowth. He wanted to avoid a plague of flies hovering around the place. It annoyed him to realize that he'd be unable to accuse a dead man of murder.

Looking around he saw that the two kids had disappeared. Worse still the box of gold had gone with them. He raised his voice and bellowed with rage.

'Come out, come out where ever you are.'

His voice roared loudly across the hills. Then, his anger vented, he reckoned that they couldn't have got far. Their two horses still grazed contentedly. Although the animals had backed off somewhat, they'd ignored all the commotion around them as they chewed on the grass. To Joaquin Mateo that meant the youngsters were on foot and hadn't gone far. He scanned the area round him. No sign of where they might have gone. Then it occurred to him that their only hiding place could be back inside the cave. He almost grunted with delight. Soon there would be two more bodies to kick down the hillside.

Joaquin Mateo vague plans to blame Luke Yale for the kids' deaths lay in tatters. He didn't care about that now. He walked into the cave to kill the two people who still separated him from his gold.

Squatting low in the shadows, Grace Warman quaked with fear. Aware that her life might soon be over, she still had the strength to fight her corner. Although Donty Moultrin had ordered her to hide away so he'd be able to take a pot shot at Joaquin Mateo, Grace decided to do her bit too. She found a rock, small enough for her to pick up, but big enough for her to be able to smash it over the man's head, and waited.

As the tap-tap of footsteps came closer, she held her breath fearful that he'd hear her. She kept as still as one of the rocks she hid against. She waited until he'd walked two feet past her and then pounced, light on her feet. Joaquin Mateo never heard a thing, but Grace heard the crack of bone under the rock as she brought it down on his skull.

Donty stood at her side a moment later. She hung onto him for support as she understood what she'd done.

'That was a fool thing to do,' Donty said.

They both looked at Joaquin Mateo as he lay on the floor of the cave a trickle of blood seeped slowly from the wound in his head.

'Very effective, though,' she said.

A surprise awaited Donty and Grace because before they had time to consider what to do about the outlaw, an Indian stepped up to them. They moved back but he wasn't interested in them. He pointed to the man who lay on the floor of the cave.

'This man killed my sister, Light Weaver,' he said.

Donty and Grace didn't argue. They had little knowledge of the man, other than that he'd been determined to kill them both for the gold. If the Indian could dispose of the problem for them, it was OK with them.

They watched as he bound the man with a thin green fibre. Joaquin Mateo made a brief attempt to struggle as he regained consciousness but the Indian brave pulled a knife from his belt and pressed it against his victim's throat. The struggling stopped and the Indian pulled him to his feet.

Soames Ho arrived as the Indian walked with Joaquin Mateo, whose feet, hobbled together, only allowed him to shuffle along. The Indian lifted the trussed up man onto his horse. Ho touched his hat and the Indian made his sign of friendship.

'Greetings, Yellow Hide.'

They had known each other for a long time. The oriental man had no argument with the redskin man but curiosity showed in his face. The Indian was in an unusually expansive mood. He pointed towards his burden.

'This' – Moon Bear said – 'is responsible for my sister's death.'

The horse neighed as he roped the man securely. He whispered a few words and the beast calmed down. He continued until satisfied that Joaquin Mateo wouldn't be able to escape.

'Are you sure he is the guilty one?'

Moon Bear bristled with anger.

'You're not going to save him from being punished for his crime,' he said.

Soames Ho held up his hands defensively. He didn't want to argue with an angry Indian. Not until he had all the facts. Although convinced that Sirrus Warman had hidden the gold and Joaquin Mateo wasn't around or he'd have been gone long ago, he decided that Moon Bear wasn't in the mood for discussion. And after all, the man the Indian captured had been involved in the robbery. As far as Soames Ho was concerned the man might have to suffer a little bit before he could help him out. And he'd know where to find him later. Nevertheless he had one last try.

'We have our own justice for murderers,' Soames Ho commented.

The Indian mounted the horse and sat behind the trussed man in one swift movement.

'So do we, my friend,' answered Moon Bear.

He touched the reins lightly and the horse, captive and rider, sped off.

Soames Ho stared after horse and rider until they disappeared and then turned to look down on an anxious pair of faces.

The two cousins, Donty Moultrin and Grace Warman, had their arms round one another and after they explained what had happened, they couldn't wait to return to Warman's Longhorn Ranch.

CHAPTER EIGHTEEN

The ranch foreman also heard the shots. He hadn't meant to follow the youngsters but he'd been sent out to help round up some strays. The map he'd seen the other night had been imprinted in his brain and he knew the shots came from the location of the gold. Eaten up by curiosity he determined to find out what had happened up there. And, well, if those kids were in trouble then Emmett Warman would be glad to know he'd been keen enough to help them.

No one was around when Al Brown turned up. He could see that quite a few horses had grazed here and their hoofs had churned the ground. He dismounted and looked about him. At his feet he saw spent cartridges from a .44 and nearby the ground coloured up red-brown. His hand went to his holster and he took out his gun. Although certain that whoever was involved in the shenanigans that had happened here was long gone, he felt safer with a piece of metal in his hand.

When Al Brown reached the mouth of the cave he cursed. He knew he'd got here too late to make a claim on the gold but he'd hoped to find something. He bent down to explore the ground. The hollows, deep and empty, were a testament to the fact that the others had been there before him and cleaned the place out.

He walked further along as he hoped to find something that would make his journey here worthwhile. The air got dank and unpleasant and he shivered as he moved further inwards. In the dark he nearly tripped over something.

'Goddamn.'

He looked down at what he thought was a pile of wood. Then he noticed something odd about it and tentatively he picked up one of the 'branches'. Al Brown shuddered as he realized the thing in his hand appeared to be a long bone. It looked like a thigh bone. He threw it away in disgust.

'Looks like someone lost their way,' he whispered. Then he laughed loudly and found where he'd thrown the bone. 'You lost your way, my friend?'

Why should he be quiet? Not as though there was anyone else round here. He knew he'd missed out.

He picked up a stone and threw it at the walls in utter frustration. The sounds resonated round the cave and cut through the silence.

In the distance someone else had heard all the noise and it disturbed him. He moved purposely towards the sounds to investigate.

Al, too busy, to notice anything amiss, kicked the ground in despair. He'd lost out all along the line and his last hope to get a small chunk of the gold had been denied him. He had travelled overland to California at the same time as Emmett Warman. They'd mined almost next to one another. Yet it had been Emmett that had struck lucky. Then Emmett had bought a ranch. It turned out to be in the best part of the county. Al Brown had tried his hand at farming but his land had been desert. In the end he'd spent his days in Emmett Warman's shadow.

When he'd listened to the two kids talk about the 'treasure', he thought his luck was in. They were so green he thought they'd churn up mud for weeks.

He noticed a lot of things, as he minded his business and went on the round-up. He'd had to be careful when he saw Joaquin Mateo in the hills, even though he had reason enough to be out there; the man would probably shoot first and ask questions afterwards. He knew him to be an ornery cuss and he was wise enough to keep well away from him. Al

Brown reckoned that if that outlaw was involved with the gold then no one had a chance. And then there was that friend of Sirrus Warman's, Lode Pinkerton. Then he had to pull back when that blasted nosy other Pinkerton man, Soames Ho, came to sniff about the place. Later on he spotted a pesky Indian poking about. It seemed as if the whole town had set about getting their hands on the buried treasure. In the end he'd decided to keep well away. Only the sound of the gunshots sparked his curiosity and made him reconsider his decision.

But even now, with everyone gone and the two empty holes in the ground, Al Brown still thought there might be a few gold nuggets left to pick up. He wanted a little slice of the wealth; something for his old age.

He caught his toe on a small rock and the unexpected obstacle unbalanced him and he pitched forward into a small crevice. Again the air turned a dark shade of blue with Al Brown's cusses.

As he regained his composure, he found himself on the floor of the cave with a pain from his foot. The pain came in waves and threatened to overwhelm him. But he was a tough old man and gingerly he felt the oddly angled limb. He judged it was broken. His anger gone, he sat dejectedly in the cave, and wondered what to do next. He knew he couldn't stay here a minute longer. He had to go. As he pulled himself to a standing position, he renewed his vow to leave the search for dreams to others; he'd just get along with plain old work from now on.

Al Brown stumbled forwards, using the long bone he'd thrown aside earlier, as an aid to help him with the gammy leg. It didn't matter now that the bone might be human. All he wanted to do was to get out as quickly as possible. As he dragged himself forward he noticed it had become much darker in the cave even though he'd moved towards the opening.

For a moment he thought perhaps he'd stayed longer than he'd thought and the sun was below the horizon. He had to move out fast; the Sierra wasn't a hospitable place at night. At least, that is, not for the likes of him now with his crippled limb. He felt a shiver ripple through his body and felt as though someone had just walked over his grave.

He wasn't usually given to fancy thoughts but Al Brown suddenly thought of the familiarity of the ranch and decided he would be content to leave the forests, mountains and deserts well alone for a while. He turned the collar of his coat up against his neck and tied his scarf tight around his neck. He felt chilly and unsettled. In fact he couldn't wait to get back out of the cave and stand in the sunshine once again.

Up ahead someone waited for Al Brown. The ears

pricked up with every sound and nostrils flared to soak in the myriad of smells which floated towards him.

Al didn't know he had a reception committee. It contained only one in number, but with the size of three men and the strength of ten.

As he made his way down the mountain side Soames Ho heard the screams. He turned and looked briefly back towards the foothills.

'What was that?' asked Grace.

Her eyes widened with horror as the inhuman shrieks filled the air. She held her jacket closer to her as if to shield her body from danger. Soames Ho shrugged his shoulders.

'A wild animal,' he said.

Grace pressed her knees into her horse. 'Gee up,' she said.

As it moved faster, Donty pushed his horse forward and caught her up.

'Race you home,' he said.

Soames Ho watched the pair as they flew, on their steeds, towards Warman's ranch.

CHAPTER NINETEEN

Emmett Warman didn't need a sixth sense to smell out trouble. His daughter Grace, who'd stamped her booted foot on the wooden porch floor, and her cousin Donty, who'd pulled his face into a grimace as if he'd swallowed a horn toad backwards, warned him all was not well. Most of all, he knew it as soon as Soames Ho followed the pair into the ranch.

Soames Ho stayed on his horse but he touched his hat and gave a little bow of his head.

'We seem to have a bit of a dispute,' the man said. 'Thought, as this pair belong to you. . . .'

'Hold it there.' Emmett put his hands up. He didn't know what it was all about but he felt he didn't have to take responsibility for all and sundry. 'This boy is my cousin's kin. And he's old enough to make his own decisions.'

'If you insist,' Soames Ho said. 'Donty Moultrin, I'm taking you into Marysville. The marshal will have something to say about you keeping the miners' gold. I think you might end up in jail for a long stretch.'

'I ain't going with you,' the youth said. 'And you ain't going to make me.'

Soames Ho pulled out his .44 Peacemaker as he spoke and aimed it square at the young man. Donty Moultrin paled to the colour of chalk. Grace, her temper settled at the sight of the gun, went to move towards him but her pa grabbed hold of her arm.

'You stay here, gal. Those two had best sort this out themselves.'

'He's not distant kin,' she challenged her pa. 'You've got to help him out.'

Emmett Warman didn't like the way the situation had shaped up, nor the comments Grace had made; they had an uncomfortable ring of truth about them. He was his cousin's son after all but he certainly didn't want Grace's life put at risk. She squirmed somewhat but he held tight and she stopped fighting him. He'd interfere if things got out of hand. At the moment, it seemed to him, the pair were just bandying words around.

'I only want what my Uncle Sirrus left to me,' Donty explained.

139

'It wasn't his money to leave,' Soames Ho pointed out. 'He stole that money from the miners.'

'That's not true.'

Donty tried to defend his uncle.

'Yes, I'm afraid it is. I saw the three men who robbed the stage. I couldn't do a thing about it' – he paused and stared at Donty and the gold – 'but now I'm going to do the right thing and return it to where it belongs.'

Trust my brother Sirrus to mess things up, Emmett thought, but he spoke out loud only to confirm what Soames Ho had said.

'You can't argue with that, boy,' Emmett agreed.

Donty Moultrin looked down at the ground to the place where his dreams had gone. They lay in granules beneath his feet.

Soames Ho looked at the dejected boy and lowered his gun slightly.

'So what's it going to be? You want to help me out?' He raised his gun again. 'Or are you going to fight me for the gold?'

Donty shook his head.

'No. You're right, mister. This money ain't mine.'

Soames Ho and Donty Moultrin set off right away. The Pinkerton Agent wouldn't stay and sup with the Warman family. He couldn't wait to finish his task, that is, to return the gold to the miners.

140

'Are you going to come back here?' Grace asked.

Donty merely shook his head. He hadn't made up his mind past the return of the gold. It took a might of thought to do that. He'd decided to shut his mind to everything beyond it.

The tour back didn't take long. They took no breaks and Soames Ho kept his sights on the green box. He hadn't blasted the lock off. The marshal could sort that out. He'd strapped the box to the wide back of a spare mule and he intended to return it as it had been sent out all those months ago.

Marysville, still the hub of Yuba County, gradually stilled as the news spread of Soames Ho and the gold's return. How the story got out, no one knew, but as they reached the outskirts of town, a trail of people were lined up ready to follow them in. Amongst them were miners. They were keen to make sure that their gold wasn't lost again. In Marysville the town folk waited expectantly.

The marshal stepped out of his law office to greet them.

'I said I'd bring the gold back.'

'You sure did.'

Everyone watched as the oriental man untied the green box from the mule. There were plenty of willing hands to unload it but the marshal stepped up to take charge.

141

'Whoa, steady,' the marshal cried over the hullabaloo. 'Let's have it in my office.'

The law office got packed with people. They quietened down and stood silently as if they all waited to draw breath. It was as if they feared the thing would disappear from sight if they took their eyes off it. Then one of the miners could wait no longer.

'Well, open the dang thing,' he shouted.

The noise level went up again.

'How the hell are we going to open it up?'

The whole crowd collectively scratched at their heads and made a noise like a multitude of mice munching through a cupboard to get the cheese.

'We got to wait until a Pinkerton Agent comes to town with a key. I've wired them to send a man pronto,' the marshal informed them.

They looked at Soames Ho.

'Hey . . . they don't give me a key,' he said.

'Don't need a key.'

A miner, fed up with all this red tape, fed some slugs into his shotgun and fired it right at the lock. The gunpowder filled the room with smoke and choked everyone for a moment. But it did the job. The lid sprang open and revealed a box which gleamed bright yellow with gold.

The marshal now held a shotgun. He knew that in

sixty seconds it could be as though a plague of locusts had flown in and eaten everything in their path. He looked towards Soames Ho for support. The oriental man nodded. Then he fired his gun into the air. The room was silent once more.

'I know you all want your money back,' the marshal said, 'and I'm going to make sure you get it. But,' he waved his gun at the crowd, 'it stays with me until I can find out who's entitled to what and to how much.'

'And how are we going to trust you, well, not you marshal; we mean anyone could steal this gold again,' said a chorus of voices.

Soames Ho picked up the box in his strong arms and went into the cell. He sat down by its side together with his gun.

'I'll stay inside with the gold,' he said.

The marshal locked the door and put the key on his belt.

'There are two people, me and my deputy, to get through first before they can get to Mr Ho. So it's safe.'

Grudgingly, the people eventually left. The marshal had got everyone who said they were entitled to the gold to give Donty Moultrin the details. As soon as it could be verified by the bank, then they'd get their money back.

The marshal told Soames Ho and Donty that he reckoned that the hills would soon fill up with gold because none of the miners had much faith in the system after this and they'd rather bury it and trust their memories instead.

The man and boy couldn't help but agree with his sentiments.

CHAPTER TWENTY

Soames Ho caught up with the Indians two days later. He saw a sight he hoped he wouldn't have to see again. Joaquin Mateo, still trussed up like a turkey, hung by his one remaining wrist and both ankles in between two trees.

He'd been through a tough time.

He felt the eyes stare at his back as he turned and walked towards the chief. Soames Ho's face didn't move a muscle. He had to be careful not to show the Indians that he felt anything for the man's plight. It would be taken as a sign of weakness.

He nodded towards the chief's son and made a sign of peace. He knew Moon Bear, and his people, well. He'd got to know them all as he travelled around for the Pinkerton Agency during the past year. It paid a man like him to have a lot of friends in a lot of places.

They respected him because Soames Ho had been a negotiator between the Indians and the townsfolk in Marysville. Unlike a lot of places, they all lived harmoniously together.

At least they used to. Since Light Weaver's disappearance and death tensions had mounted. Whereas the ranchers had been able to rely on the Indians to help with the work, they now had to look elsewhere for labour. And workers were hard to get when most people still panned for gold and dreamed of the fortune to be had with a lucky find.

Soames Ho, or Yellow Hide as they called him, had done them some favours and he wanted to draw them in. As he'd have expected to return any favours done for him. So now he asked them for a thank you for his help. The process was slow. It couldn't nor shouldn't be hurried. Soames Ho respected their traditions.

They all sat round the fire and the calumet, the peace pipe, was passed from one man to another. The ceremonial pipe helped to unify the group of men and let them speak together as friends. Soames Ho realized he was about to risk a lot if things went wrong. There was only so much good will in the world. He didn't want to rush things but Joaquin Mateo wouldn't last that long left to hang in the tree

146

and soon the Indian braves, fuelled by the feast and the firewater, might decide to torture their prisoner again.

'I know you believe in justice. So I come to ask, not for myself, but for this man,' Soames Ho said.

He looked towards what was left of Joaquin Mateo.

The chief and members of his tribe looked puzzled.

'Why should you help this scum?' Moon Bear snarled. 'He killed our sister Light Weaver and now he is being punished.'

The others agreed with him.

'I don't believe he is the guilty man,' Soames Ho explained.

Moon Bear jumped to his feet. He held a knife in his hand. The dry blood that clung to its blade probably belonged to Joaquin Mateo.

'Do you accuse me of speaking falsely, Yellow Hide?'

Soames Ho remained cross-legged on the ground. He did not make a move to stand up to Moon Bear. The action would have looked too aggressive.

'You know that in my job as a Pinkerton Agent I ask questions.' He looked towards Moon Bear and the chief. 'I made some enquiries which makes me believe that Joaquin Mateo wasn't there when your sister was killed.'

147

'So who is the man who killed her?' the chief asked.

Moon Bear, his knife still held tight in his palm, cautiously sat down again. Soames Ho, grateful that they held him in high enough esteem to listen to his words, continued.

'Unfortunately, the man is dead. Sirrus Warman, who is Emmett Warman's brother, hid the gold. When he arrived at his brother's ranch, he was so wounded from a gun shot that he died within less than two weeks. His brother had no knowledge of his crimes.'

'We must make his brother pay for the crime,' Moon Bear said.

The chief spoke to his son.

'Emmett Warman has always been a good man. It's his brother that is rotten. We can't hold that against him.'

'I don't know how it happened but Light Weaver was murdered and then laid in the ground, side by side with the gold. It wasn't by the hand of the man you have here.'

The chief put his hand on his son's arm.

'We can't kill a man who is innocent.'

Moon Bear looked at the dancing flames and then towards Soames Ho.

'And is this man innocent?' he asked.

148

'Joaquin Mateo is guilty of many things, but not this.' Soames Ho continued to speak when he saw hesitation in the red man's eyes. 'Let's come to an agreement that will suit us all.'

With the deal agreed by all, Soames Ho walked over to Joaquin Mateo. He cut the man down and trickled some water over his lips.

'You come to free me?' croaked the dying man.

His glazed eyes focused on Soames Ho.

'The tribe must be satisfied that justice is done,' Soames Ho replied.

'Take me with you,' Joaquin begged.

He looked at the man with compassion. Then he shook his head.

'They will allow me to make sure you suffer no more.'

Joaquin Mateo's eyes flew open at the words. Then he realized he had no more options.

'Make it quick,' he said. 'I've been in this world too damn long.'

CHAPTER TWENTY-ONE

'It comes with its own reward,' the lawman said.

The marshal had been through this charade once before. He spoke of the money attached to the return of the gold.

'Don't want it.'

Soames Ho lived a simple life. He had what he needed and didn't see the sense in being weighed down by a surplus of anything.

'You could give it to the school, I suppose.'

The marshal had heard of the oriental man's generosity. He'd caused a stir offloading the cash he'd got for bringing in his folks' killers.

'I hear that schoolmarm, Annie Greames, has done a lot of good things with that money.'

'That was the idea,' Soames Ho said.

On several occasions he'd seen the improvements she'd made and approved the prudent way she'd spent the money. He conjured a vision of the young woman who taught in the school. Perhaps he ought to call in and say hello. Then he mentally dismissed the idea. He didn't want any attachments of any kind. He recalled the loss of his family. Attachments caused too much sorrow.

'How about that young lad, Emmett Warman's nephew?' the marshal continued.

The lawman didn't want to look after the reward. It soon caused trouble if folks got to know there was money hanging around. Soames Ho looked as if he might consider it. He nodded his head.

'I'll speak to the kid,' Soames Ho promised.

Privately, he wondered if the boy would even speak to him, let alone accept it. Donty Moultrin had thought he was heir to a small fortune but it had proved to be a pig in a poke. And the girl hadn't come off too well, either. Her pa hadn't taken kindly to the near loss of a daughter and had forbidden her to leave the ranch.

Soames Ho could see a filly that was straining against the bit. Perhaps her pa hadn't seen that Grace Warman was full-grown and wanted her own adventures. He smiled and wondered if he ought to suggest that the girl could do worse than marry her second cousin and make her own nest. On reflection, Soames Ho couldn't see his suggestion would be well received. He decided to keep his opinions to himself. It didn't do to interfere too much in other folks' lives.

He stood up, brushed down his dark-wool jacket and checked his guns and knife were secure. The marshal watched his actions, and remembered a long time ago the young man who'd vowed never to be armed again. But things changed, he supposed, and a man had to uphold the law and at times make sure other people upheld the law as well. Soames Ho took his leave of the marshal and decided he'd have a drink in the saloon before he called at the Warman's ranch. Then he would call into base in California and see what the Pinkerton Agency had lined up for him. He could send a telegraph but he fancied a break from everything and a slow ride across to California, with its warm and pleasant climate, would suit him fine.

Although he'd decided not to call into the schoolhouse he couldn't ignore the school marm when he nigh on bowled her over as they bumped into each other on the sidewalk, after he'd finished at the bath house.

'Are you all right, miss?'

152

His arms went round a well-padded woman; that is, she was padded in all the right places. He helped her to her feet. When he noticed her blush, Soames Ho released her to give her a moment to compose herself. But he needn't have worried. Annie Greaves proved to be made of sterner stuff. He saw her face crinkle into a smile and heard a merry laugh fall from her lips.

'Nice to meet you again, Mr Ho,' she said.

Soames Ho supposed a woman who could deal with a room full of boisterous youngsters would be able to deal with most things.

'I didn't expect it to be quite as nice as this,' he said.

'You got time to come over to the schoolhouse? The children are finished for the day.'

It was on the tip of Soames Ho's tongue to say no, but another look at the lovely lady made him decide it was worth a minor delay.

'I've got new slate boards for all the children,' she said.

She walked around the schoolhouse and pointed out all the improvements she'd had made. Soames Ho watched her animated face as she continued to tell him about the material items she'd purchased with the money he'd donated, and about the progress the children had made and showed him

153

samples of their work. It delighted him to look at her face. He was sorely tempted to enrol in classes so he could watch her all day.

They drank coffee together and ate some home-made cookies. When she invited him back for supper he ruefully took his leave.

'You'll come back, Soames Ho?' she asked. 'When you're next in town, I mean.'

The oriental man made no commitment.

'Maybe,' he said. 'Maybe.'

After he took his leave of Annie, Soames Ho rode out to Warman's Longhorn Ranch. He wondered if he hadn't already made arrangements to sup with the Warmans whether he'd have succumbed to dine with a very lovely lady. On reflection he decided it was for the best. Perhaps it was best to avoid attachments with anyone. Far too complicated, he'd decided.

Tonight didn't hold much to look forward to, he thought, as he neared the ranch. The two kids had made plans, which they knew they ought not to have, but then youngsters always did, he supposed, and he'd ruined their daydreams. He decided that as soon as was polite, he'd make his excuses to leave.

As a sop, in the saddle-bags under his thighs, he'd stored the reward money. That might ease the pain. Grace Warman had more than enough luxury in her life, but Donty Moultrin hadn't had it so easy. The reward might well put a smile on his face. In fact, Soames Ho knew it would. And that took the awkwardness of the visit away.

The reaction didn't disappoint him. Donty Moultrin's eyes grew huge with pleasure.

'So, what are you going to do with all that money?'

Grace's willow-coloured eyes widened as well. For a moment they reflected the green monster within her. Then it vanished and her sweet nature took over.

'You could do so much with all that,' she smiled.

'Invest it, boy.' Donty's Uncle Emmett had a practical streak. 'Don't waste it.'

Soames Ho could see the myriad of emotions etched onto his face. He waited to see which side of the boy's personality would win through.

At last Donty said, 'I'll send most of it to Ma. And bank the rest.'

'That's a sensible boy,' Emmett said. 'Send enough to get my cousin over here with her kin. That's where she belongs.'

Donty shook his head sadly. He didn't think his ma would uproot herself and cross the wilderness to live amongst men who had 'gold fever' and 'heaven knows who'd murder you in your beds'. Mary Moultrin had a fixed view on life that would keep her horizons narrowed forever.

'I don't know whether that will happen, sir.'

Outside, after supper, when Soames Ho and Emmett Warman drank whiskey and smoked cigars at the supper table, the two youngsters sat on the porch together.

'You're some goody-goody,' Grace teased her cousin. ' "I'll put all my money in the bank, sir".'

Donty grinned from ear to ear at her mimicry.

'Well, I'll put some of it in the bank,' he said, 'but doesn't mean I can't get it out again.'

'You want company to help you spend some of it?'

Donty looked at his young relation. She certainly was an attractive girl. She'd make someone a wonderful companion but he couldn't see that set-up as something he wanted right now. And he figured that Emmett Warman wouldn't accept less than a gold band on his daughter's hand if she left his ranch with a man. Donty Moultrin believed anyone who offered less or tried to take advantage would have some serious problems to contend with. He imagined that peering down the barrel of a gun might be high on the list.

'No.'

Donty answered her question abruptly. He didn't like the fact that her smile faded away but he decided he'd best be truthful and straight with her. They were both too young to get hitched.

'I might ask to tag along with Soames Ho. That is, if he don't mind, and I want to go and explore California.'

Grace tried to pull her lips into a smile but the smile didn't quite reach her eyes.

'I wish you the best of luck,' she said.

He pulled her towards him and placed a kiss on her lips.

'I'll probably come back this way someday,' he said.

Grace broke from the embrace and her eyes flashed.

'Donty Moultrin, don't you think I'll be standing here on the porch waiting for you,' she said.

'I'm sure you won't,' he agreed. 'But if you are. . . .'

They kissed again.

Inside the ranch, Emmett Warman puzzled over the foreman's disappearance.

'Ain't known Al Brown wander off before,' he said. 'Not in all the years I've known him.'

Deep furrows appeared in the older man's brow. Soames Ho thought for a moment.

'There's been a lot of talk about gold these past few weeks. You think he might have gone to look for some?'

Emmett puffed out his cheeks and pulled his

mouth into a grimace.

'Can't imagine it,' he said. 'Bit long in the tooth for digging for gold in the hills.'

Suddenly Soames Ho felt a chill. Those sounds he'd heard roll over the mountains. Well, he didn't want to think about it too much.

'You don't think he might have decided to follow those youngsters and look into the cave?' he asked.

Emmett chuckled.

'You know, that's just what he might have done. Always ready to take a look at something he shouldn't. Damn well ought to have been an investigator like you.'

Soames Ho hesitated then decided to share his misgivings.

'I heard some awful unholy screams up there,' he said. 'That cave belonged to a bear. Might not have taken kindly to all the people who'd tramped over its domain. Your Al Brown might have caught unlucky.'

'Think I'd best take a look in the morning,' Emmett Warman said.

'If I were you I'd leave it until spring,' Soames Ho advised. To make light of it all, he added, 'And who knows, he might walk back in at any moment.'

'You're right. No sense in worrying about it. He'll be fine.'

The two men looked at each other and neither

believed it to be true.

Soames Ho and his young companion, Donty Moultrin, left early the next day.

'Make sure you do come back this way,' Grace Warman said.

She looked full at Donty as she said the words. He smiled back at her.

'You bet I will,' he assured her.

'And you call in, Mr Ho, if you're in these parts again,' Emmett Warman said.

Soames Ho touched his hat.

'You bet I will,' he echoed.

Del M.
2